Two Sides

Lisa Lije'

Two Sides

Lisa Lije'

GEMLIGHT PUBLISHING LLC

Southlake, Texas

ISBN: 978-1-7367934-7-3

Gemlight Publishing LLC
2600 E. Southlake Blvd.
STE 120-377
Southlake, Texas 76092
gemlightpublishing.com

Ordering Information:
Special discounts are available on quantity purchases by corporations, associations, and other groups. For details, contact the publisher at the address above. For orders by U.S.A. trade bookstores and wholesalers please contact Big Distribution:

Tel.: (833) 436-5483

or visit gemlightpublishing.com.

Printed in the United States of America.

Dedications

To my supportive family, near and far, for your continued prayers throughout this journey.

A very special thank you to my cousin, Aerrial, for believing in me and pushing me to no limits.

"I can do ALL things through Christ that strengthens me" (Phil 4:13).

Prologue

LaShae knew from the moment that she spilled coffee on her brand-new blouse and had to change right before she walked out of the door that her day was already ruined.

About an hour earlier, Keven had arrived at her office with a bouquet of roses and chocolates in hand which was never a good sign. In school, Keven, better known as "Flash," was the sexiest and most well-mannered boy on the basketball team. He was also the fastest on the football and track team. Every girl hated the fact that he only had eyes for one girl, LaShae Moniiq Wilson. They hated her for being his and tried everything to sabotage their relationship. Because LaShae, Shae for short, and Keven had such a bonded trust, it made it all a bit easier to handle. Keven was a rising basketball star, heading to college and then the NBA; however, he broke not one, but both of his legs on a senior ski trip and could never recover on the court. Now, years later, he was still angry at himself for going on the senior class trip. He was now seemingly known as a "has been" and a blue collar worker.

LaShae took the gifts and placed them on her desk. She then waited for Keven to tell her the real reason for his unexpected visit. Keven shifted nervously as though he was being forced to say what his intentions were. It was almost as if someone was watching him.

"Shae… baby, we need to talk," he finally stated.

Confused and worried, LaShae sat in the chair behind her desk. "What's wrong, bae?"

Present time:

All she heard was the sound of a car horn coming from behind her. She glanced in the rearview mirror only to see the impatient driver waving his fist in the air.

As she pressed on the gas to move forward, everything went dark. And then…

Chapter One

La Shae

NO! NOT AGAIN

It was 5:35 a.m. when LaShae was finally able to focus. She noticed that she wasn't at home nor was she at her mother's and she became a little frantic — rightfully so since she could not remember how she got there.

"Where am I?" LaShae asked, trying to focus on the stranger sitting in the chair next to her bed.

"Thank God, you're awake," said the stranger. "I have been praying that you were okay."

"Who are you?" she inquired as she tried to sit up to face this *praying* person. Her entire body ached. "What happened?" LaShae's throat felt like it was on fire, but she had to know what was going on. She had to get it out. So she asked again, "What happened? Why am I here?"

"To answer your first question, you are in the hospital. Secondly, my name is DeTroyt Maning, but you can call me Troy," he said with a smile. "It's nice to meet you, Miss Wilson." He held out his hand to shake hers but quickly realized that she was in too much pain to move it.

"Wait. Hospital?" She wanted to scream those words, but she was still in too much pain! With what she could muster out, LaShae asked, "What am I doing here? Where is my family?"

Troy got up from the chair and made his way over to the window. As he stared out into the beautiful sunrise, he felt a sense of relief just knowing that LaShae had made it through this ordeal.

LaShae could see tears glistening on his face. Not phased at all, she asked "Are you crying?" Troy apparently didn't hear her so she asked him again. This time, her voice was just above a whisper.

After what seemed like an entire century of silence, DeTroyt finally spoke. "I'm the reason you're in here."

Trying hard to remember what actually happened, LaShae sat up and focused on what he had just said. She did what she could to ignore the pain that she was feeling, but at the same time, she had to make sure he said what she thought he said. "Did you just say that *you* are the reason that I'm here?"

"Yes, I did," he replied as he turned to look at her.

"What are you talking about?" She was trying to stay as calm as possible, at least until he said what it was he meant.

DeTroyt turned to face her, looking very concerned. His eyes never left her gaze as he said, "I crashed into you at the intersection. Don't you remember?"

Confused, LaShae said, "No! No, I don't remember. How did… or better yet, *why* did you crash into me? Did you not see me or something?" Not only was her throat still burning from forcing words out, but her entire body felt like someone used it as a punching bag. "Can you please help me get me some water? My throat is awfully dry."

He made his way back to her bedside to assist her with the water. Afterward, he took her hand into his and looked her straight in her face. "Yes, I saw you, Miss Wilson. But I had to do something. I couldn't just let you run out in front of that 18-wheeler. It's almost as if you were forced out into the street." He looked at her and she looked as though she had much to say. "I wanted to stay with you just to make sure you were okay."

"Are you sure you're not just hanging around *pretending* to be nice so that I don't sue you?"

Ignoring that accusation, he said, "I'm extremely sorry, Miss. Wilson. I know that there is nothing I can do to make you forgive me…"

"You right, there isn't!" she said, interrupting his poor, apologetic speech, at least that's what it sounded like to her.

"But with all my heart, I am truly sorry," he continued, ignoring her remark. "You have to believe me. I never meant to hurt you. I was only trying to help you." DeTroyt spoke very softly and timidly. It was almost as if he were a child confessing to eating that last chocolate chip cookie that his grandmother told him not to eat.

"Help me?" she choked out while screaming those same words on the inside. "Does this look like you've helped me? Do you actually think that you can just come in here and charm me with your tears and your sorry excuse for an apology speech and think everything is okay? I'm so over the charm! How is being hooked to this monitor helping me? Huh?" There was a slight pause before she continued. "You know what, DeTroyt Michigan? You—"

"Maning," he corrected.

"Whatever! You've cost me a lot by putting me in this dungeon with no *real* explanation as to why you crashed into me in the first place. I can't work here. I can't pay my bills here. I can't take care of my son here… Oh my God! My son! Where is my son?" Panic took over as she feared the worst… him being left at the daycare all this time. LaShae began to tackle the IV in her arm and every other plug that was connected to her body, trying to get out of bed to get dressed. "I've got to get my son. Oh no, he's been there all night long."

At that moment, she felt DeTroyt grab her arm. "Please, Miss Wilson, get back into bed. You're not ready to—"

"Take your hands off of me!" she almost screamed. "Who are you to tell me what I am and what I am not ready for? This is all entirely your fault anyway! You're just being nice to me so that I don't sue you! But guess what? It won't work! Now, get out!"

Oh, no… I feel …I…

Then everything went dark.

LaShae awoke to find her mother standing over her. Jasmyn Gibson owned her own boutique shop and carried her independence very well. A lot of people called her "Jazzie" because, well, that was just how she carried herself. She didn't like trouble makers, and her sassiness refused to take any junk from any man. The ladies at her shop were always talking about her fair skin, her long beautiful black hair, and her 5'8" frame that carried a shape out of this world.

I guess that's where my features come from. I inherited everything from my mother except her attitude toward men. I give them way too many chances, and I always end up getting hurt in the end. Jasmyn Gibson? One time and one time only, if luck is in their corner.

"Mama, what happened?" LaShae's voice was so faint that had Jasmyn not been so close to her, she would not have heard her.

LaShae had to admit that her body felt as if it had been used as a punching bag. She ached all over, especially in her head. "Where's Kaleb?" she managed.

"He is at your grandmother's," Jasmyn responded. "Don't worry, honey, he's fine. He has been asking about you though, but I've assured him that you were okay and that you would be home soon."

"Thank you. That's good to hear," she said, trying to smile through her tears.

Jasmyn enlightened LaShae on some things that Granny was going through and how LaShaes's accident reminded her of when her cousin, Clifford, had his motorcycle accident and died. Granny stories could scare the life out of a person.

Even though LaShae heard every word that Jasmyn said to her, her mind was focused on one thing, her mother's facial expression. It must have shown on LaShae's face because Jasmyn got very quiet. Even though she was smiling, LaShae could see right through it. "Mama," she started, taking her hands. "I know you are worried about me, but really, I am okay. I just got a little shaken up when I thought Kaleb was still at daycare, especially when *that* guy told me that he was the reason that I was in the hospital in the first place. Where is he anyway?" she asked, looking around the room.

"Where's who, baby?" Jasmyn questioned.

"That man!" she snapped.

Smirking, Jasmyn answered, "Oh, *that* man. Well, Troy went to get us some breakfast and—"

"Troy? Mama you know him? Better yet, you're gonna let him come back in here after what he did to me? I can't believe you! What kind of mother are you?" *Yup, I was in for a rude awakening.*

"An extremely grateful one!" The look on her face made LaShae regret what she had just questioned of her. Had she not been in the hospital already, she probably would be wishing she were right about now.

"Now you listen to me young lady, Troy saved your life! Yes, he may have inconvenienced you for a little while, but it's better than not having you around at all." Her voice was shaky, but her eyes were still strong. Still, she knew her mom was deeply hurt by her words.

"What are you talking about, Mama?"

"Baby, Troy collided into you on purpose."

"On purpose?"

"Yes, Shae. He did it on purpose."

"I'm confused. Why would he purposely hit me like that?"

Jasmyn began pacing the floor and finally stopped in front of the window. After staring out for a minute or two, she turned to face LaShae with tears in those eyes that moments before were so strong.

Taking a deep breath, she said, "You see, sweetheart, there was an eighteen wheeler that was loaded with explosive chemicals headed straight for you as soon as you pulled off to make your turn. The truck driver was at too high of a speed to stop at the red light that he was racing against. As it happened, Troy was there and saw what was about to happen and was able to cut you off in the middle of your turn, causing a collision between you and him instead of you and that truck."

She took a deep breath, then continued her story again. "That truck, however, was able to stop a few hundred feet after your collision took place. The driver came back to check on the two of you to make sure no one was badly injured or worse. Troy told him that you would be okay and that if he wanted to leave a name and number, he would call with any news of your well-being. So the driver, realizing everything was under control, left the scene. *That man* risked his life for you, someone he doesn't even know. Aren't you aware that had it not been for *that man* that God placed in your presence at that particular moment, you wouldn't be here?"

A hot flush inched up LaShae's face as tears welled up in her eyes. "I feel like a total idiot, Mama. All I did was argue with him and yell at him. Why didn't he explain that to me in the first place? Well… actually, I really didn't give him a chance to say much because I was so angry. I guess I owe him an apology, huh?"

LaShae looked up to see her mother gawking at her in awe because she hardly ever admitted when she was wrong. But in such a case as this, when she was wrong, she was wrong.

"When is he coming back anyway?" she asked.

At that moment, the door to her room eased open and DeTroyt walked in carrying what looked like bags of food from every chain in the city. Through angry eyes, LaShae never knew how handsome he *really* looked. Of course, he would never hear that from her.

"Ah, I see we're finally awake," he said, grinning from ear to ear. "You really gave us quite a scare, Miss Wilson."

I know I'm not gonna admit this to him, but he has the most gorgeous and bright smile I have ever seen. Oh, and he has super straight teeth too.

"Yes, I am definitely awake," she responded, smiling back. "Listen, Mr. Maning, I really need to talk to you".

"Okay, but please call me Troy," he stated. "Do you want to eat your breakfast first?"

"No, thank you. Um, Troy… I'm really not hungry and this really can't wait until after breakfast. Mom, do you mind giving us a moment?"

"No, honey, that's fine. I need to get to the office anyway. I know that you need to discuss some things so I'll call you later, okay?" Jasmyn began gathering her belongings.

"Thanks, Mommy. I love you, and I will definitely talk with you later." LaShae gave her a hug and Jasmyn kissed her cheek before leaving.

"What about your breakfast, Ms. Gibson?" Troy held up the bags.

LaShae smiled as Jasmyn took the bags from Troy and gave him a hug. "Thank you for breakfast. We'll have to do this again." Looking around the room, she added, "Of course, in a different setting. Take care okay?" With that, she left the room.

Troy pulled up a chair next to the bed. LaShae tried to get comfortable, but found it difficult to do so in such a tiny bed.

Looking at her out of curiosity, he asked, "So what'd I do this time, Miss Wilson?"

"Please, Troy, call me Shae. All of my friends do."

"Oh, so we're friends now?" he said. It was more of a statement than a question. "Okay, Shae, to what do I owe this act of kindness?" he asked curiously as he began to eat his breakfast. "I hope you don't mind. I'm starving."

LaShae waved it away and silence filled the room. She took a long time to gather her thoughts so that she wouldn't sound like a complete idiot when she finally opened her mouth to speak.

"Well, my mother explained the accident to me and how you saved my life. I feel like such a fool. All the while you were trying to make sure that I was alright, you didn't once complain about your pain and all I did was cause you drama. I don't know how to thank you. I mean, I've been such a jerk and…"

"I don't want to hear it, Shae!" he said in a very firm tone while holding up his hand to stop her.

"What?" She was in complete disbelief. "What do you mean, you 'don't want to hear it'? I have gathered up the nerve to even look you in the face to apologize but you don't want to hear it?"

"Are you finished?" he asked, still eating his breakfast.

"No, I'm not! You have some nerve! Here I am, trying to be nice to you, and…" She trailed off and went blank. She couldn't think of anything to say or call him. *What?*

"It seems as if you are finished now," he said knowingly. "Are you?"

"Yeah, and so are you! Goodbye!" LaShae pointed toward the door. She only wished that she could open it and push him through it.

"Whoa, hold on there a minute," he stated, surprised at her actions and holding his hands out in front of him in defense. "Why are you putting me out like that? Don't you even want to know why I said that?" Troy leaned in closer to her so that he could look directly into her eyes.

Oh my goodness. He is so cute!

"No, I don't want to know," she replied, turning her head to break the gaze.

Using his forefinger to turn her face back to his, he stated, "Well, I'm gonna tell you anyway." He leaned back in his chair and continued. "I want to look at you and thank God that He put me there on His behalf to intervene. I'm grateful that you are lying in this hospital bed versus a casket. I don't even take that route home in the evenings because of how terrible the traffic is. So yes, it was all God. I don't want your apology, even though those are the nicest words you've said to me since I've been here. I just want you to get better. Will you do that for me?"

She nodded yes and he patted her on her hand.

"Are you a reverend or something like that?" Her lingering eyes did not leave where his hands were.

He let out a little giggle. "No, I'm not. But I do love the Lord."

"Mmm, okay."

"Well, I've gotta run. I have to help get the church ready for service tomorrow. I will check on you tomorrow." He slowly began walking toward the door as if he were waiting for her to say something.

So, she did.

"You go to church, huh? What are you? Baptist or something? Pentecostal? Catholic? What?"

Troy obviously wasn't expecting that question and the shocked look on his face proved it, but he turned to address it anyway. "I believe that the Word of God is true all by itself regardless of what denomination I am." With his hand on the doorknob, he continued. "Listen, I really gotta be going, but once you get out and feel up to it, I hope to see you at service one Sunday."

There goes that smile again, she thought. "I'll have to take you up on your offer. What's the name of your church?" she asked, really not enthused, but entertaining him. *I really want to know, but at the same time, I'm trying to figure out if I really want to go. I don't think I'm ready for all of this, but I would take the information just in case I change my mind later.*

Troy reached into his pocket and pulled out a business card. He flipped it over. "This is the name, the location, and the phone number of the church I attend. On the back, I jotted down all of my numbers in case you decide to come one Sunday and need a ride or something."

She graciously took the card and thanked him before he turned to leave. Something he said before he left really stuck out. He told her to hurry up and get well because she had work to do when she got out of here.

I wonder what he meant by that? He's not all that bad, just not my style. He's a good fit for somebody, just not me.

Chapter Two

DeTroyt

THE WARNING

Troy stood on the other side of the hospital room door with a pleasant smile on his face. "Thank you, Lord. Mission accomplished," he stated as he looked up toward Heaven.

As he waited to get on the elevator, his cell phone rang. Troy looked at the display for a moment, puzzled, because the number displayed was *private*. He usually wouldn't answer, but for some strange reason, he did.

"Hello?"

"You got what you wanted?" The voice coming across the receiver was low and distorted.

"Excuse me?" Troy answered, taken aback.

The low and distorted voice repeated the question.

"Who is this?" he asked, a bit agitated.

"Don't you worry about it, pimp. Just don't go getting your little church drawers in a knot over that pretty little princess you caught yourself saving yesterday. She is off limits to you and anybody else that tries to get close to her. You got it? She's mine, pimp! I got my eye on you."

Before Troy could respond to those allegations, the caller disconnected. He looked at his phone in disbelief, with all sorts of thoughts running through his mind. *Should I go back and warn LaShae of this conversation? Of this person?*

The ding of the elevator door drew his attention back to where he was. Instead of going back to LaShae's room, he got into the elevator and pressed the button for the lobby. After getting to the lobby area, he quickly scanned the area for anyone that looked suspicious. He stood there for a moment, thinking of returning to LaShae's room for clarity, but he decided against it. Troy walked out of the lobby and into the parking garage toward his vehicle, a smoke gray Range Rover. As he got closer, he noticed a yellow sheet of paper stuck under his wiper blade. He removed the note and opened it carefully. The words, "STAY AWAY FROM HER!!!" was written in bold red letters.

Troy scanned the parking lot and assumed this was the same person who called him minutes before. He didn't see anyone, so he cautiously walked around his vehicle, looking over every inch of the Range Rover and its 22" chrome rims. He checked his tail pipe, each tire, and even under the hood. "You can never be too careful nowadays," he said to himself. After inspecting the vehicle, he proceeded to get into the driver seat of the Rover, and that was when he saw it. A dark figure quickly walking away. Troy called out to the figure who in turn, started running.

"Ok, enough is enough." He jumped into his Rover, started the engine, and sped out after the running figure. "This is going to end right now!"

After getting onto the main road from the parking garage, Troy saw the figure running and then ditching into an alley. Troy swerved into the alley after it. There was nowhere else for this person to run. Troy threw the Rover into park and jumped out, running full force toward the figure.

With one swoop of the leg, the figure, now smaller than before, fell with a thud to the concrete street. The guy called out in pain.

"Who are you?" Troy asked. He was now straddling the figure who Troy realized was actually a boy that looked to be at least sixteen years old.

The boy was dressed in a long trench coat, blue jeans, white tee, white sneaks, and a plain black cap. He looked to be about 5'6".

Troy had now grown impatient with this kid, who again, had refused to answer him. Instead, he tried to spit in Troy's face. Lucky for him, Troy saw it coming and ditched.

"Who sent you kid? What is your name?" Troy yelled, gripping the boy tightly around his collar.

"Buzz off!!" replied the boy.

Troy stood up, pulling the boy with him. "Well, we'll just see if you say that to the police."

"Okay, okay," the boy replied. "Not the police."

Troy kept shoving him forward toward the Rover.

"I said I'd talk!" The boy stiffened in his stride, catching Troy off guard.

"Look," the boy started. "I don't know who the dude was and I didn't get a good look at him, but he paid me $50 bucks to put the note on your windshield."

"What do you mean you didn't get a good look at the guy?" Troy questioned, obviously not believing him. "It's broad daylight!" he yelled. "Tell me everything and don't you leave out one thing! You hear me, kid?"

Troy shoved him into the truck from the driver side, got in himself, and closed the door. He put the truck in reverse and pressed on the gas.

"Hey, man, where are you taking me?" the boy asked, now appalled at the entire situation.

"We're just riding right now, but lie to me, and we go straight to county."

"Alright! Al-right!" he replied, holding up his hands in surrender. "I'll tell you everything."

Chapter Three

Jasmyn

A THIEF AMONG US

It was extremely busy at the office when Jasmyn arrived. "Wow, it's good to know that business is booming. Thank you, Jesus!" Her boutique really needed these sales to make it through.

As soon as Jasmyn got into the elevator to press the button for the 2nd floor, she felt something was wrong. No sooner than she stepped off, she heard the sound of heavy feet running toward her. It was her first assistant, Jake. Jake was like the private eye of Gibson Jewelry and Designs, Jasmyn's Boutique. Nothing, absolutely nothing, not even a kitten's purr on a stormy day got past this guy. He was so nosey that he could be a lead detective. Of course, no one liked him because they felt he kissed up to the boss (and he did)… Jasmyn was glad to know that someone, other than herself, had respect and concern for herself and her company.

"Boss lady! I think you need to see *and* hear this!" He hurriedly escorted her in a direction opposite her office.

"Well, can I get into my office first, Jake?" she asked, a bit agitated.

"No, ma'am. This is important. We caught a theft on video. This happened around midnight last night, and you may want to know who it is."

"What? Oh my God! I'm right behind you." Jasmyn was in total disbelief. "Who in the world would want to steal from me?"

When she and Jake entered the conference room, Jasmyn saw her co-owner, Miranda Jones, MJ for short, one of four security guards that also worked for Jasmyn, the QC personnel, and two police officers.

"Miranda, what is going on?" she asked.

"Well, Jasmyn… um…"

MJ, a very nice young lady with a big heart, had been Jasmyn's right hand since day one six years ago. She was normally always feisty and ready for a duel but not today. It seemed as if the cat had her tongue and just wouldn't let it go.

Her pudgy nose and full lips brought out her moon-shaped face. Her deep brown skin and short brown and honey blonde streaked hair showed off her almond shaped eyes. She was as tall as Jasmyn, 5'8", with a nice figure, but it was not helping her out today. When Miranda continued to stumble for words, Jasmyn asked again.

"Can somebody please tell me what these people are doing here?"

"Ms. Gibson," said one of the officers, taking over the conversation. "It seems that Ms. Jones will be taking a ride downtown with us. We were waiting until you got here before we booked her."

"Book her! MJ? What is he talking about?" Jasmyn turned back to the officer. "Why are you trying to arrest her?"

The second officer turned to Jake and nodded for him to start the video that was already pre-set. This would show exactly what the commotion was all about. He turned back to Jasmyn and said, "Now, Ms. Gibson, let's just see how trustworthy your *business partner* really is," he stated, pointing toward the projector screen.

"What?" she questioned, astounded by the officer's remark.

The video began to play and what was on the screen was unbelievable. Miranda was closing down for the night, which was normally around 10 p.m. The video surveillanced MJ in the vault where the most expensive jewelry and cash were kept. She went in with no bag, but came back out with a black sack in one hand and a money bag in the other. Miranda carefully placed the bags in a box that she had stashed away under her desk. She waited until the last person left the boutique to load the items in her car which she had parked in the alley behind the boutique after lunch. She was almost in the clear when a security officer, who was making his rounds, caught her loading things into her car. After that, he began questioning her and then calling the police. When MJ tried to weasel her way out, that was when the video was replayed to her, showing her every step. MJ cringed at the thought and realization of what her friends were going to say.

After the video was played, Jasmyn was trying hard to wake up from what seemed like an awful nightmare. Unfortunately, she realized that she was never asleep. She held back the tears and did not give into the pain that she was feeling at that present moment. Instead, she discussed it with MJ. She felt her knees go weak and found the nearest chair to sit in.

"Miranda, how could you? How could you steal from me? I took you in when you didn't have any place to go."

Remembering this, Miranda dropped her head as Jasmyn continued. "I gave you a roof over your head, food to eat, and half ownership of *my* business, *my* fantasy, *my* dream, *my* hard work! I thought you were better than that!"

"That's the thing, Jas," she said, looking back up at Jasmyn. Tears were now streaming down her face. "It was always yours, yours, yours, and never ours. Isn't that what partnership is all about?" Miranda asked. "Well, isn't it?"

Jasmyn responded in a calm, but stern voice. "No, that is not what a partnership is all about. Partnership is about trust, honesty, and understanding. I thought I had that with you, MJ. All these years and you were just setting me up for this." She turned to the officers and said, "Officers, I don't care what you do with her or where you take her, just so long as she's out of my face *and* this building. And please hurry up before you arrest *me* for aggravated assault."

Jasmyn grabbed her things to head to her office, but not before the officer responded to Jasmyn's threat.

"Now ma'am, we don't need you to make those kinds of threats toward Ms. Jones. I would hate to have to shut your business down by putting you behind bars as well."

"I would have to do more to her than make a threat for you to shut me down. My business goes nowhere, but as for her, get her out of here now," she said as calmly as she could.

"Yes, Ms. Gibson. Come along, Ms. Jones. Let's go." Miranda was read her rights as she was being escorted out of the building.

With that, Jasmyn turned and walked out of the conference room and rushed to her office. She hoped that no one heard her as she closed her office door and began to sob uncontrollably.

By noon, the phones were ringing off the hook. Every reporter in town had gotten a whiff of the attempted robbery and Jasmyn was just about fed up with it all.

Jake had gone to Jasmyn's office to make sure that she was okay when the phone rang. "Who is it now?" she questioned staring at the phone. "Jake, could you please answer the phone for me? If that's another reporter, I'm gonna scream."

"Sure, Ms. G."

He then turned to pick up the phone. "Gibson's Jewelry and Design, this is Jake. How can I help you?"

"Hi Jake! It's Shae."

"Hey, Shae! Ooo girl, let me tell you. Your mother—" Jake began.

"Hey, baby," Jasmyn said, as she snatched the phone from Jake. "Don't mind Jake. He's running, trying to catch up with his mouth again."

Jake rolled his eyes at the comment.

"So how are you, baby?"

"Mmm, a little better. My head finally feels normal again. The doctor says that if my blood pressure stays down, which I have been doing a great job with, I can go home later this evening."

"Oh, honey, that's great! Just let me know and either myself or Jake will be there to pick you up."

"Ok, Mama, but I didn't call to talk about me. Mama, I heard what happened today. It's all over the news. I'm very sorry, really I am."

There was a slight pause, a deep breath, and finally she spoke. "Thank you for that. Sometimes the people you try to help and even the ones you love the most always have a knife waiting for you somewhere down the road."

"Are you okay, Mama? I'm sorry, I shouldn't have brought up the subject."

"No, she stole from me and it really hurts right now. Well, I have some work to catch up on, but we can talk about it later. I just need to get over the shock. Get you some rest. I love you," she said, sounding as strong as she could.

"I love you too, Mama. Bye."

"Bye, baby." Jasmyne hung up the phone and sat back in her chair. "What in the world possessed MJ to do such a thing?" she asked out loud to no one. "I don't understand. Wasn't she happy here? I thought I had given her everything and yet she stole from me."

Jasmyn has never been robbed before, and she sure as hell didn't grant any employees access to anything in the building but Miranda. Then she remembered the surveillance tape.

"Jake," she buzzed. "Can you get me that surveillance tape from the burglary again?"

"The police took it for evidence when they left." Jake replied. "What's the matter, boss lady?"

"Nothing," she lied. "Thank you." She didn't want to let Jake in on her plans until it was the right time. She wanted it all to go away, but knew in her heart that this was just the beginning.

"Lord, you've got to help me get through this."

Chapter Four

Detroyt

THE POLICE STATION 1:57 P.M.

Troy had finally made it to the church, but he could not keep his mind from wandering about the things that had transpired hours before. With finding the note on his car and not to mention his encounter with the young man, who he later found out was named Jared, a runaway from a local group home.

As he continued working around the church facility, Troy also thought about the phone call that he received prior to chasing down Jared in the alley.

"Who was that man and who was he to LaShae? An ex-boyfriend or husband? What is she not telling me?" he asked out loud.

Soon, everything was done and everyone was leaving the church. The lawn and bushes were neatly cut and trimmed. The pews, pulpit podium, and communion table were polished. The bathrooms were cleaned, trash cans were emptied, and the carpet was vacuumed.

Troy said his goodbyes until tomorrow's service. He then jumped into his Rover and left.

The police station was about ten minutes away from the church, but because he was going to the hospital to see LaShae afterward, he thought it would be best to go home first to shower, shave, and change. Forty-five minutes had passed and Troy was finally ready to make his presence known at the precinct.

When he arrived at the police station, a call came in from Jasmyn's office. He quickly answered, thinking something may be wrong with Shae. "Hello?"

"Hi, DeTroyt, I mean Troy. This is Jasmyn," she replied.

"Yes, what can I do for you? Is LaShae alright?" he asked.

There was a slight pause, then she continued. "Yes, she's fine. I need you to do me a favor."

"Sure. What is it?"

"LaShae called a little while ago and said that the doctor may release her today or in the morning as long as her blood pressure is stable. When she does, is there any chance that you can pick her up from the hospital and take her home for me? I will call you with the address to take her to when she calls me. I have some things to take care of here, but I also want to give her a surprise coming home party."

Troy had to think for a second before making such a commitment, but he finally said, "Sure, Jasmyn. Just let me know. Listen, I really need to take care of something right now, but just call me as soon as you find out when she's ready." He didn't want to rush Jasmyn off the phone, but he felt a change of subject coming.

Sounding uncertain, she answered, "I will and thank you so much."

"You're welcome. I will talk with you soon." With that, he ended the call and turned his focus back to the mission at hand.

He rushed up the stairs of the precinct and through the double doors. He walked up the desk, note in hand, and asked to see a detective.

"May I ask what this is about, sir?" responded the lady behind the counter. She looked to be in her late 40s, but looks can be deceiving nowadays.

"I have been followed, threatened, and had this note left on my car. I don't know this person nor do I know how he got my number or knew where to find me. I need to find out who this is immediately. Now, may I please speak with a detective?" He realized the clerk was just doing her job and instantly regretted his tone.

"What is your name?" she asked.

"DeTroyt Maning," he replied.

"Mr. Maning, please wait right here." She scurried off to get a detective and came back with a heavyset, dark haired gentleman by the name of Detective Jones.

They introduced themselves to each other and Detective Jones requested that Troy follow him to his office.

Detective Jones pointed to one of the three chairs planted in front of his desk as he closed the door behind them.

"So, Mr. Maning, you have received threatening phone calls and you found this piece of paper under the windshield wiper of your car. What do you think triggered this to happen? Do you have any enemies or frenemies that you are aware of?" he asked jokingly, but quickly saw that Troy was annoyed.

"Listen, Detective, I was in a car accident less than 48 hours ago. The girl that was involved is in the hospital recovering. I went to see her after the accident and actually stayed with her last night just to make sure that she would be alright. Her mother came by shortly after we got there yesterday evening after picking up her grandson from daycare, so I volunteered to stay with her overnight."

Detective Jones sat back in his chair and crossed his leg over his knee, seemingly puzzled. "Yeah, I heard about that. So you're saying that you don't know this girl at all?"

"Exactly. Before the accident, I never knew that she existed. The only reason that I hit her was to save her from being plummeted over by an 18 wheeler carrying explosive material. The driver was going too fast to stop at the red light, and it was either the city block or her and me. I chose the latter. I haven't done anything to anybody."

"Is this all in the police report, Mr. Maning?" asked the detective, who had now sat back up in his chair and was leaning forward. "It seems to me like you interfered with a mission, but I don't want to speculate…"

"Wait, so you're saying that that truck was supposed to hit her?" Troy began to rewind the accident scene in his head and then it hit him. "I gave that trucker my information, but he would not give me his… he just left the scene."

"Did you get a tag number, truck number, anything?" asked Detective Jones.

"No, I did not. I was so concerned about getting her to safety that it didn't cross my mind."

Detective Jones raised an eyebrow. He wondered how Troy could be so thorough with his notes but forgot to get that bit of information.

"Well, Mr. Maning," Detective Jones stated while standing to his feet. "If everything is in the report, then we will find out who the person is. I mean, we are not sure if this guy intentionally tried to run her over and is upset because you interfered, or maybe he is someone who is innocent in the whole matter. Whoever he is, we will find him. I will definitely keep you posted. What hospital is the young lady in?"

That question made Troy kind of uneasy, but he knew at some point, he had to trust somebody. "She is at IG Memorial Hospital, room 321," he finally responded.

"Ok, then. I will head that way in a little while to speak with her.

Maybe she can give us a lead on the situation."

Troy extended his hand to the detective and thanked him for his help. All the while in the back of his mind, he knew that he had to get to LaShae before the detective did. He hurried out of the office and back out through the double doors where he entered twenty minutes earlier.

Getting into his car, he noticed yet another note. This time when he opened it, he saw that the note was written with cut out letters from a magazine and newspaper clippings. *"I AM WATCHING YOU, MR. MANING!"*

His first intention was to go back into the police station and show Detective Jones what he had just received; however, he decided against it. He would just show it to him when he came to the hospital this evening. Right now, he knew he had to get to LaShae.

Chapter Five

La Shae

DOCTOR'S ORDERS

The rest of the day went by quickly. The nurses were in and out of LaShae's room, checking her vitals to make sure that her blood pressure was within normal range.

"This bed is so uncomfortable, and I am *soooo* ready to go," she complained to one of the nurses.

Instead of responding to her complaint, she continued to busily do her job with a smile. "The doctor will be in to see you in just a moment."

The nurse was gone for a few minutes before returning with the doctor. Because of the look on his face, LaShae already knew that it was *not* good news.

"But, I feel fine, Dr. Nelson," she protested.

"Just because you feel good, doesn't mean that you are good," Dr. Nelson replied. "Your blood pressure and creatine numbers are still elevated, so we would need to keep you for at least another 24 to 48 hours to monitor you."

"24 to 48 hours?"

Dr. Nelson laid a calming hand on her shoulder. "I know this isn't what you wanted to hear, Miss Wilson, but it is for your own good that you are here. You were in a very bad car accident, and it's a miracle that you are still alive."

His words rang true in her head, but she was really not trying to hear what he had to say. And the nurse that she had complained to, not even 20 minutes earlier, had the nerve to have a smirk on her face. LaShae opened her mouth to say something else, but all she could say was, "I know." She then reflected on the conversation she had with her mom earlier.

As soon as the doctor and nurse left the room, LaShae couldn't help but cry. Just thinking of another day away from her Kaleb did not sit well with her.

She called her mom to give her the news. Jasmyn also agreed with Dr. Nelson. "It's for your own good, sweetie. Don't worry, I will bring Kaleb later. Get some rest."

"Yes, ma'am. I will try."

LaShae then called MyChele, her bestie, since she hadn't spoken to her since Friday. "Hey, girl. How's it going?"

MyChele screamed so loudly that LaShae's ears were ringing. "Hey, girl! I'm doing well. But how are you? How are you feeling? Girl, we got so much to talk about." MyChele went on and on about her weekend and LaShae told her about her having to stay a little longer in the hospital. They laughed a little and cried a little.

Fifteen minutes had passed when LaShae heard a knock at her door. "Girl, somebody just came to my door," she told Mychele. "Let me call you back, okay?" They ended their conversation.

"Come in."

"Knock, knock. Peekaboo, guess who?" came a familiar voice.

"Peekaboo, guess who? What? I do believe I'm a little too old for nursery rhyme games." She had to laugh at his attempt. "Why are you here anyway? Did my mom send you to check on me?"

"Well, I just came to see you," he answered as he sat in the same chair he had the day before.

"Oh, how sweet of you," she replied. Looking at the expression on Troy's face, she frowned. "This is not a social visit, is it?"

"I was hoping that you can answer a few questions." He reached into his pocket and pulled out both notes and handed them to her.

She look at the notes curiously. "DeTroyt, what is this?"

He looked at her in the same manner. "I was hoping that you could tell me," he started. "They were left on my car. The first one was left on my windshield in the parking garage this morning when I left here and the other one was on my windshield when I left the police station reporting about the first note as well as the phone call I received this morning"

"A phone call? What kind of a phone call?" This had caught her completely off-guard and now she was worried that someone was watching her.

Troy settled back into the chair as he gave the entire story, including the bit with Jared. By the time he was done, LaShae was in such disbelief. "Why would anybody want to hurt you? Because of me?" She pondered that question, trying to see if she had made any enemies along the way, but no one came to mind.

"The detective that I met with at the station, Detective Jones, is coming by to speak with you about it this evening. I told him about the accident and the driver of the truck. He was wondering that maybe the driver's intention was to hurt you, but since I intervened, it made him very angry at me."

"And what about this Jared person?" she asked, more curious now.

"Jared is only 16 years old, but because of his height, he could pass for at least 20. He ran away from a group home across County Line. He said that they were doing awful things to the children. He wasn't going into detail but just said he couldn't take it anymore."

"But what does Jared have to do with the notes and the phone call?" LaShae asked impatiently. She wanted him to hurry up and get to the point and stop beating around the bush.

"Well, because Jared has been panhandling on the street, this person that Jared calls 'Big Guy,' extended an opportunity to him. 'Big Guy' told Jared that he could make decent money if he did what he wanted. In other words, be his pimp. So Jared agreed and got fifty bucks for the notes. The only thing that is puzzling to me is I took Jared to a secure place. So how did another note get placed on my car at the police department?"

They both pondered that thought. "Does that detective know about Jared?"

"No! And I want it to stay that way. We need to find out what's going on and why." Troy could tell that she was a little uneasy by the tone in his voice. He gave her an apologetic look before addressing it. "Look, I'm just trying to figure out what is going on." He got up to pace the floor. "Why, all of a sudden, after your accident, are you being followed? Who are you, really?"

"Are you serious right now? You're questioning me?" LaShae didn't know how to take that. "I'm just as lost as you are on this, Troy. I don't know what's going on either. Maybe 'they' are trying to use you to get me. "

"Yeah, maybe," was all he could say. DeTroyt's phone began to ring, and he immediately sent it to voicemail. The phone rang again. Same number. DeTroyt again, more agitated, sent the call to voicemail. This time, the caller left a message.

Reaching for his phone, LaShae asked to hear his voicemail. "I want to see if I recognize the voice."

DeTroyt wanted to hear it too even though he was hesitant. He scrolled through his voicemails and clicked on the most recent one. Immediately, she cringed after hearing the voice. "Turn it off. Please, just turn it off."

"Do you know this person?" His eyes never left hers, but she couldn't answer him.

She couldn't tell him about her past. He mustn't know. Stephon Johnson was back and it appeared that he meant business this time. "But it can't be him," she whispered. "Why is he here?"

"Huh? Who is here? LaShae, who are you talking about? Who's after you?"

She could hear the frustration in his voice, and she didn't want to upset him no more than he already was.

She couldn't afford to let DeTroyt in on this just yet. She knew he was being harassed, but she just couldn't tell him right now. "DeTroyt, I can't—"

"Yes, you can, LaShae," DeTroyt interrupted. "Please, I need to know."

"No!" she said firmly. "I need to rest; my head is starting to hurt again. Please Troy, let's not talk about this. Please."

"We may not talk about it now, but I'm not going anywhere either. Detective Jones will be here any moment now. So if you're not going to tell me who it is, are you going to tell him?"

"No, Troy!"

"Fine! But I'm not leaving until after Detective Jones leaves."

LaShae could tell by his tone that he was very frustrated with her, but she didn't care. She could not let him get involved in this. It was too dangerous.

Thirty minutes had passed with no further conversation between them, then there was a knock at the door. DeTroyt looked over to LaShae who had fallen asleep and realized that he must've fallen asleep also. He opened the door to find Detective Jones standing there and instead of inviting the detective into the room, he quickly insisted on them meeting in the hallway instead in fear of "disturbing" her rest.

"Detective Jones, it's good to see you again," he whispered.

"Likewise, Mr. Maning," he replied. "I assume that the young lady is asleep? Is this the reason why we are out in the hallway?" he asked, eyeing DeTroyt curiously.

"Yes, she is. I wanted to speak with you alone."

They found an empty waiting area not too far from LaShae's room. Once they sat down, DeTroyt cut to the chase. "Listen, detective, I came over here to check on LaShae, but while I was here, he called. I sent it to voicemail because I didn't recognize the number. Well assuming it was him, he called right back and I sent it to voicemail again. This time, he left a message. She wanted to listen to the message, so I let her. When she heard his voice… " DeTroyt's voice trailed off.

"What happened?"

"It's as though she heard the voice of a ghost. I tried to get her to tell me who it was, but she didn't want to discuss anything with me. She turned her back to me all the while saying, 'No, it can't be… it can't be,' until she fell asleep."

Detective Jones listened intently, but finally concluded that he really wanted to speak with LaShae before he left. DeTroyt didn't think it was a good idea, but he knew that Detective Jones wouldn't give up nor leave the hospital until he did, especially now that he knew the circumstances.

Reluctantly, they went into her room. Detective Jones tried multiple times to talk to her, but he finally gave up after she refused to say anything. He told DeTroyt that if she mentioned any names or gave a description of the person, to please notify him as soon as possible. DeTroyt agreed and the detective left.

DeTroyt stayed with her until the next morning before church. The nurses had been coming in and out of the room all night to check her vitals signs which had in fact elevated some. With the way that everything went, he wouldn't be surprised if they kept her for two more days.

Chapter Six

La Shae

HOME AT LAST!

Sunday came and went for DeTroyt. He enjoyed Sunday service and left on a spiritual high, forgetting everything that happened since Friday. "Ahh, Monday morning."

No sooner than he got those words out, his phone rang. Looking at the display screen, he saw that it was Jasmyn and answered.

"Good morning, Troy."

"Good morning. Is everything ok?"

"Yes, all is well. Remember that favor that I asked you about? About picking up LaShae from the hospital?"

"Yes, I remember. What time will she be ready?" he asked, trying not to let her hear the tiredness in his voice. He had been up all night thinking about everything that happened, and he finally was ok for the most part of the morning until now. He knew that he gave Jasmyn his word, and now it was time to hold up to it.

"She said that she would be ready later this afternoon. Maybe around 4ish. I am planning a huge coming home party for her, so you picking her up for me would be a great help. I know she's going to ask why I didn't come, so be prepared." Jasmyn let out a little giggle before thanking DeTroyt and ending the call.

He went through the rest of his work day anticipating what this evening was going to bring after his encounter with LaShae. Before he knew it, it was time to go home, well at least for the other workers.

DeTroyt made it to the hospital around 4:30 that afternoon, and just like Jasmyn expected, the questions began.

"Where is my mother?" she asked. "She said either she or Jake were coming to get me."

"They're both at the office. I guess what happened to your mom took a deeper toll on her than she expected."

"You heard about that too, huh? I don't understand how someone so bright and talented as MJ can take from the one that helped her get to that point," LaShae said as she sat up on the edge of the bed.

DeTroyt shook his head in agreement and began gathering her things. LaShae rushed over to open the door and accidentally bumped into him, causing him to drop the bags and trip over them. She had to laugh to herself before offering her assistance.

"Here, let me help you." LaShae didn't know what it was, but when she touched his hand, she felt something; he must have felt it too because he quickly pulled away.

"I think I can manage," he quickly responded. "Just open the door *before* I get off the floor, please." The tone in his voice sounded a little embarrassed, but he had to laugh. At least she knew he was not angry with her… well, not yet anyway.

The elevator ride was quiet, which gave her the opportunity to really take in everything that had transpired over the last few days. She noticed that DeTroyt seemed a little bit more relaxed than he was on Saturday. She noticed his posture as he carried her things. She didn't have a lot of bags and they weren't heavy, but his posture was perfect. He did not slouch nor did he complain about having to carry them.

She watched his facial expression. Something about it made her wonder and want to ask him what he was thinking, but she figured silence was best right now. LaShae did, however, continue to admire what was before her. He was clean shaven and had a goatee that fit perfectly around his round-shaped caramel face, not to mention his lips and smile. His eyebrows were thick and even, and his eyelashes fit his almond shaped eyes that appeared to be light brown in color, just the way God intended. Perfect! Everything about this man was perfect, including his body. She had to think of something to say before her imagination got the best of her.

"So, how did you know to come and pick me up?" she asked even though she already knew it was her mother's doing.

Once they reached the parking garage, he checked the surroundings as they walked toward his vehicle.   "After you called your mother, she called me and explained why she couldn't pick you up and asked if I could. So… here I am."

"Yes, I see. Thank you for going through so much trouble for me. I mean, you really didn't have to."

"You know, what, LaShae?" he started as he began putting her things in his Rover. "You're a very nice person when you're not being Ms. Feisty-all-Mighty."

"Ms. Feisty-all-Mighty? Excuse me?" She shot him a look.

"See what I mean?" He started laughing so hard at her that he almost didn't realize a car was coming their way. "What the—" he exclaimed, pushing her out of the way.

"Who the he—" LaShae started.

"I don't know, but we're following them! Get in the truck!"

They started out toward the exit when all of a sudden, another car pulled out in front of them and threw on the brakes. It was almost as if to stall them so the person who just tried to run them over could get away.

"Troy!" yelled LaShae. "Would you please watch where you're going? Haven't we had enough accidents?" The moment the words left her lips, she felt regretful.

"Oh now, that was a low blow, LaShae. You didn't see what just happened?" he shot.

"Apparently, *you* didn't!" she shot back.

"Haven't I suffered enough from your insults?" He clearly had enough of her smart mouth at this point. Not only had the driver in front of them not pulled off, but LaShae actually yelled at him again. She figured that he was about to go and find out what was wrong when he reached for the door handle, but instead, he blew the horn. The driver lifted his head to the rearview mirror and suddenly sped off. DeTroyt and LaShae both rode in silence for a few minutes, and then…

"*You* suffered?" she asked in amazement. "What about me? I had to relive my entire accident all over again!" Without realizing what was happening, LaShae felt warm tears rolling down her cheeks.

"So you *do* remember?" he asked without even a glance in her direction. It almost seemed as though he hated that she did remember.

"Yeah. I… uh, I guess I do," she replied over the lump in her throat.

"So what exactly do you remember? If you don't mind me asking."

"Do you really want me to tell you what I remember? Better yet, let's just change the subject. I'm still a little edgy about the accident and then to almost be plowed down? I'd rather not talk about it, okay?" She sighed before giving this last bit of information to him. "I do want to know one thing. My mother said that the truck driver came back to see if I was all right. Did he tell you what his name was?"

DeTroyt, now looking at her with concern, answered, "No, he didn't."

"Look, that person is probably long gone by now. I just want to go home."

No further discussion about the accident took place, and they finally arrived at Jasmyn's boutique. LaShae couldn't wait to get inside.

After greetings from the staff, she finally arrived at her mother's office. It was a beautiful place that she had taken the time to decorate herself. Jasmyn received a great deal of compliments on her craftines which was displayed throughout the entire building; however, this spot, her office, her solace, was the best of them all. She was even offered a great sum of money by a guest to be her personal decorator. Jasmyn would've taken her up on the offer but that would mean leaving her business for long periods of time without proper supervision. So, of course, she said no.

DeTroyt and LaShae met Jasmyn in the hallway of the second floor. She was smiling from ear to ear when she saw them. She welcomed LaShae with open arms.

"Oh, my baby! You still look so weak and pale still."

"Mama!" she hissed.

"Well, you do. Where is your lipstick, child?" she asked while examining her face, snickering to herself.

"Mama, you're embarrassing me. I just got out of the hospital, so how do you expect me to look?" LaShae said through gritted teeth. "I applied what little makeup I had with me to at least look alive, but I see that didn't help much."

"I'm sorry, sweetheart," she said as she continued to snicker. "I'm just not used to you looking so plain."

Jasmyn then turned to DeTroyt. "And how are you today? I really want to thank you for taking the time to pick Shae up for me. You just don't know how much you've helped me out. How about coming over for dinner tonight as a payback for being so generous?" she asked him, ignoring LaShae's body language.

"Mom, what are you doing?" LaShae asked under her breath.

To Shae's advantage, DeTroyt declined her offer, mumbling something about a prior engagement at the church. LaShae, in her mind, feels that a man going to church that much meant he was either trying to impress somebody or he was hiding something. *I really don't know what it is about me, and this church thing, but maybe one day…*

Her thoughts were interrupted when her mother nudged her on the arm.

"Shae, are you okay? You've been in la-la land since DeTroyt turned down my dinner offer. Don't tell me you're disappointed."

"No, Mama. I'm not disappointed," she said, rolling her eyes. "Are you ready to go yet?" she asked, trying to change the subject. "I'm starving."

"I was just finishing up when you all got here. Give me a minute to gather my things then we can leave."

While Jasmyn gathered her belongings, LaShae went to the restroom down the hall to see how bad she *really* looked. According to her mother, she looked bad enough to scare a black cat on Halloween.

LaShae looked in the mirror and scared herself. *Oh my God, Mama, you were right. I do look plain and that's an understatement. My goodness, my hair…* She tried to retouch her makeup and stuff, but what was the use now? She had been seen already.

She headed toward one of the stalls; once inside, she heard the bathroom door open and the voices of two ladies.

One of the voices LaShae recognized because she talked often when she came to see Jasmyn, but she couldn't quite make out the other voice. They were discussing the incident between Jasmyn and MJ.

"Girl," started the unrecognizable voice. "I heard MJ stole over $100,000.00 worth of jewelry and was about to get away with it too until that new security guard — you know the real nosey one — caught her."

"You mean they actually have a security guard that works and pays attention?" came a familiar voice. "Do you know what I could do with that kind of money?"

"Well, let me tell you this, Jackie. Out of all the employees that are here, MJ was the best one that Jasmyn had. She never raised her voice at us or hung over our shoulders all day long asking what we were doing and how much more work we have to do, ya know? I mean, I honestly hate what happened to her, but if you do wrong, good things won't come to you."

LaShae heard shifting as they both did what they had to do in their own stall. She then heard toilets flushing and water running afterward.

Then, they continued their conversation.

"Diane, you know that MJ was getting tired of getting short changed by Jasmyn, right? She would say all the time how Jasmyn only used her to open this shop and get her business off the ground. One day, MJ overheard Jas on the phone telling somebody that she was gonna fire MJ because of her 'lack' of cooperation and that she didn't deserve one thin dime of this business because all she was… was a body in the atmosphere."

"What?" Jackie asked, mouth opened and eyes wide in disbelief.

"Yes, honey," continued Diane. She had to pause for a minute because of the automatic hand dryer. Once it shut down, she started up again.

"So MJ told me that she decided to take what belonged to her before everything went down. That's why she did what she did. It wasn't to hurt anybody; she just knew that she was not going to get a piece of the business that she helped build, that's all. Her fair share, you know?"

Jackie, now opening the door to leave, questioned why Jasmyn would even think about letting MJ go, let alone not giving her a portion of the business that was rightfully hers.

"Hmph, you know how these rich girls are. They think that they can have anything they want, treat people like crap, and get away with it."

"Hmmm," was all that Jackie said.

As LaShae listened to the restroom door close and Jackie's and Diane's voices fade in with the rest of the crowd, she inched her way out of the stall. Angry, hurt, and confused, she began washing and drying her hands. By the time she got into the hallway, Jasmyn was waiting for her with folded arms. She didn't know what to say, so she gave a weak smile and headed toward the elevators.

The ride home was awkward and quiet, mainly because of what she overheard in the bathroom. LaShae guessed Jasmyn figured that she was tired and didn't really want to talk, which was true, but she still could've asked something.

"Surprise!"

She was indeed surprised. It appeared Jasmyn had invited everyone that she could think of for this welcome home party. And guess what? Even Troy was there. *Didn't he tell my mother he was going to church?*

Before she could make it to him, she was surrounded by a squad of people hugging and kissing on her, saying that they're glad she's okay and *blah, blah, blah.* Then, she heard a little voice she never thought she would miss so much.

"Mommy! Mommy, you're home!" Kaleb came running through the crowd, almost knocking people over to get to her.

LaShae welcomed him with open arms and tears of joy. "Kaleb! Oh, sweetheart, I've missed you so much."

"I've missed you too, Mommy. I'm glad you're home. Big Mama was getting on my nerves," he said, making a face.

Though LaShae corrected him for saying that, all she could do was laugh to herself and hold him as tightly as her strength would allow. "Well, sweetie, you don't have to worry about that anymore. Mommy won't leave you like that again."

"Promise?" he asked, making an X over his heart.

LaShae repeated the motions. "I promise." Just looking into that beautiful face with those gorgeous long lashes made her wish that she could give him anything his heart desires. Not because he wanted it, but because he deserved it.

LaShae's thoughts were interrupted when she felt a tap on her shoulder. She turned to find Troy standing before her, looking rather handsome in his "church" attire. *I guess he did go after all.*

"Hello, LaShae. Glad to see you and Ms. Gibson made it home okay." He turned to Kaleb. "You must be Mr. Kaleb." He extended his hand for Kaleb to shake. "It's nice to finally meet you."

"How do you know my name?" Kaleb asked with a funny-looking

expression on his face.

DeTroyt smirked. "Your mother spoke a lot about you when she was away."

"Really?" His entire little face lit up at the thought.

"Yes, she did."

There was a brief silence and then Kaleb asked, "How do you know my mommy?"

Before DeTroyt could answer, LaShae replied, "Well, honey, this gentleman saved your mommy's life."

Kaleb looked at her with an expression she'd never seen before. "He saved your *life*, Mommy? What's his name? I want to tell everybody who saved my mommy!"

"Uh, Kaleb, I don't think he wants his name out there like that. I—"

"It's okay," DeTroyt interrupted. "My name is DeTroyt."

"DeTroyt? Like Detroit, Michigan?" Kaleb asked with very curious eyes.

DeTroyt smirked as he thought back to his first conversation with LaShae. "Yes, like Detroit, Michigan except it's spelled with a 'y' instead of an 'i.' You can call me Troy for short. Deal?"

"Deal, but why did your mama name you that?" Kaleb asked in a curious little boy's way.

LaShae's face became flushed with embarrassment. "Honey, go play, okay?"

"But Mom!"

"Kaleb, now."

"O-kay." Kaleb took a few steps before he turned around to thank DeTroyt again for saving his mommy's life.

"Troy, I am so sorry. Really…"

"It's okay, LaShae, really it is," he assured her as he took both her hands into his. He looked as though he wanted to say something more but thought better of it. He inched his face toward hers and for just that split second, there were only the two of them in that crowded room. As she closed her eyes and positioned herself for the greatest moment of her life, she was disappointed by a quick peck on the forehead. "Look,

I need to be going. Get you some rest and I'll check up on you tomorrow if that's okay with you."

Her heart was still racing from the excitement and disappointment. "Y-yeah, uh sure."

After he said his goodbyes to everyone, she felt like a complete idiot. *How could I think he would have wanted to kiss me?*

"LaShae Moniiq Wilson!"

She turned to see her best friend, MyChele, pushing her way through the crowd toward her. She hasn't seen her since before the accident. MyChele was pretty decent though. She had to be in order to hang around LaShae. Her parents put her through law school, bought her her first BMW, and paid for her apartment while she was going to school. Of course, she had to keep her grades up in order to keep all of that. She stood about 5'9" in stature. She was a little stubby, but not too big.

"Hey girl!" she yelled, waving her hands in the air as she raced toward LaShae from across the room.

Oh yeah, did LaShae mention ghetto? People often let MyChele's professional look fool them.

"Girl, who was that hunk of a man you were just talking to? And then smacked you on your forehead? Don't tell me you've broken up with Kevie."

"MyChele, did you have to mention Keven in my moment of happiness? To answer your question, I didn't break up with him, he broke up with me."

"What?" she said, giving her a look of disbelief, but at the same time, relief. "When?"

"The day of my accident. Actually, right before I left work, he called me."

"You mean he wasn't man enough to face you? Why that low down dirty, good for nothing, selfish, son of a—"

"Hey, it's alright. Look, I'm extremely tired. Do you mind if I call you later? I'm really beginning to feel woozy and light-headed."

"Shae, you have all of these people here and..."

Before Mychele could finish, LaShae was climbing the stairs

to make her departure announcement. "Excuse me. May I have your attention please?"

The room fell silent.

"Okay, I really would like to thank each and everyone of you for coming out to welcome me home. To my mom for putting it together, I love you and thank you so much. I hate to be a party pooper and a disappointment, but I'm really tired and would like to get some rest. Please stay and enjoy yourselves. I'll see you all again soon. "

Everyone was very understanding and waved their hands in her departure. She waved in return then continued upstairs to her room. *Finally!*

"Yes, you will see me again, Ms. Wilson. Yes, you will."

Little did LaShae know, her nightmare had only just begun…

MyChele decided to follow her up to her room anyway. She didn't really mind, but at the same time, she wanted to be alone.

Once behind closed doors, LaShae begin to go on about how stupid she was for thinking she was going to be kissed by this man. "Oh my goodness! How could I be so stupid as to think he would actually kiss me? I feel like such an idiot. I hope I didn't give myself away with that *look* I gave him."

"Girl, don't worry about that," said Mychele. "I'm quite sure he wanted to, but he just didn't know how you felt about it. Did you see how he looked at you? How his eyes just lit up when you smiled back at him? And did I mention he was fine?"

LaShae had to laugh at that statement. "Girl, yes. You've mentioned that he's fine to me several times. If he gets any finer, I'll be in trouble. He's a church boy though, and you know how I feel about them."

"Huh? What do you mean I know? How is that?" she asked, sounding confused. "They are human too, church or not. Everybody makes mistakes. We're not all perfect you know."

"I know, Chele, it's just… well, never mind," she said, deciding to drop the subject while she was ahead.

"Look, Shae. I know Keven was your first love and all, but you need to get over him and move on. Especially after what he did to you..."

LaShae watched her as she propped up in the bed and flipped the channels on the television. "Ooo girl, this is my show. Look at her, she thinks she's all that with her big house and fancy car." MyChele was referring to the character on television. "She just doesn't know that her husband is at another woman's house right now." After a minute of silence, she finally turned to see why LaShae hadn't said anything about her comment. She only saw tears.

Why do I let that... that name... that person... that maniac get to me like this? I'm so embarrassed to be crying over someone who doesn't even love me and probably never have. For eight years, I gave everything to him. My all, my life, my time... and not once did I ever cheat or even think about cheating with anyone. Yet, he turns and does this to me? It's not fair, and I really don't appreciate it.

The thoughts were running through her head so rapidly, she didn't notice MyChele getting off the bed until she heard her door slam shut. Shae looked up to see MyChele standing there with her hands on her hips.

"I'm sorry, girl, but I had to do that. You were *waaaayyyy* out there. I've called your name at least six times and you never replied. Where were you? In another galaxy?" She walked back over to the bed and sat down next to LaShae. "Now that I have your attention, why are you crying so much? It better be because you didn't kiss that fine man tonight and you really regret it because if it's over Keven, I will push you out of your own window."

Shae couldn't help but laugh. "Girl, you are crazy."

"I may be crazy, but I made you smile. Now spill it. I want to hear everything so you can get it out of your system. You can't be breaking down like this, girl, that's crazy!"

LaShae looked at her in amazement. "Are you sure you want to hear *everything*?"

Mychele sat for a minute or two before replying. LaShae guessed she was debating on whether or not she really wanted to know about it all. Finally, she answered, "Yes."

"Okay, get comfy because this will take a while."

"Goodness, girl! What happened? Don't tell me he abused you because I won't tolerate it," she said, sitting up and giving her a mean-mugging look. "I mean, I know we all grew up together and everything, but I will hurt him!"

"MyChele! Just listen, all right?" LaShae continued, not up for the drama.

She repositioned herself on the bed so that she was comfortable. Unaware of what may come out of her mouth, MyChele braced herself for the dark side that she never knew.

About an hour passed before MyChele could get a word in. LaShae's face was soaked with tears by the time she was finished and wadded up tissues were piled up on her bed. Both of their eyes were extremely red and swollen.

MyChele was looking at her best friend with wide eyes as tears streamed down her cheeks. MyChele stood up and began to slowly pace in circles and then stopped to look at her. After a few minutes, she was able to utter some words. Words that she knew would cost her the sister/friend bond that they had since the 7th grade.

Without hesitation, she began. "LaShae, there's something you need to know." MyChele never called her by her whole name unless it was important. So LaShae braced herself for whatever bomb MyChele was about to drop. Afraid to ask what it was, LaShae just waited until MyChele was ready which was all too soon for her.

"LaShae, you said there was one incident where Keven left for two days and you had no idea where he was."

LaShae didn't respond. She only stared at her, waiting for her to continue.

"I knew where he was because... because..." Her words trailed off as she looked into her best friend's eyes. Her thoughts began to muddle together as she tried to figure out what to say next.

"Because what, MyChele?" LaShae's tone even startled herself. *She better not even say what I think she's about to say because if she does...* "Because, what, MyChele?!" she asked in a more authoritative voice.

MyChele looked at LaShae with hurt in her eyes.

"Get out! *Get out!*" LaShae yelled. "I don't ever want to see or hear from you again! As far as I'm concerned, as of this day, this hour, this very minute, this very second, our relationship is dead! Do you hear me? *Dead*, MyChele! Now get the hell out of my house!"

MyChele pleaded for LaShae to listen, but she wasn't hearing it. "LaShae, you don't understand. Please let me finish."

"You are finished, now get out of my house!"

MyChele left without hesitation and tears were streaming down her cheeks.

Apparently, the noise reached downstairs because Jasmyn ran in shortly after MyChele left.

"Shae, honey, what happened? What was all that yelling about?"

LaShae couldn't do anything but cry on her mother's shoulder like a little girl that just broke her favorite toy.

"It's okay, baby. Whatever it is, it's all right." Jasmyn rocked her back and forth until LaShae dozed off.

Chapter Seven

DeTroyt

PRAISE HIM

Arriving at church after service had started was not what DeTroyt had planned at all. He was never late, but he just had to stop by to make sure that LaShae was doing okay.

"Well, I'm here now," he mumbled under his breath.

He was greeted by Deacon Barber, one of the newest deacons who had come to the church a few years before. Deacon Barber was in his early 30s. He was tall, slim, and bald. His wife, Helen, never seemed to leave his side — rain, sleet, or snow. She was very supportive, not only of her husband, but to the ministry of the church as well. That was the type of wife DeTroyt was looking for. Someone dedicated to God first and then him, but so far nothing came into play.

"Brother Maning, how nice of you to make it. We've been waiting on you."

DeTroyt was surprised at that statement. "Waiting on me? For what?"

Deacon Barber just smiled. "You'll see once we get inside. Come on."

Mother Sarah grabbed his arm and pulled him through the doors of the church. To his amazement, there was a sanctuary full of church friends and family. The pastor was sitting in the pulpit, talking with the other associate ministers. The room fell silent once DeTroyt walked in.

Sharmaine, a 15-year-old girl, who had a little crush on DeTroyt, ran up to him and hugged him so tightly that he could hardly breathe. "Mr. Maning, I'm so glad you're okay! You had us all so worried, especially since we… Well, I haven't seen you in a while." She gave him an innocent wink.

"Hi, Sharmaine. It's nice to see you too," he said, forcing a smile. "Where's Vicki?"

"Vicki? Um, Vicki is, uhh…"

"Excuse me, Sharmaine, but I think I can answer his question myself. Run along now."

DeTroyt turned to face the familiar voice that he'd never thought he'd hear again. To his surprise, it was an old friend from high school, Carla Sanchez. She and DeTroyt used to date back then, but after graduation, she left without a trace — no forwarding information or anything. Later on, he found out from Carla's sister that she had gotten married to some rich lawyer out in Ohio. *Why is she back here after all these years?*

"Hello, DeTroyt. It's good to see you again," she said with a warm smile and opened arms.

DeTroyt tried to give a convincing smile, but it did not work. "Carla, you haven't changed a bit," was all he could manage to get out. He did not mean that statement as a compliment at all.

"Look, D, you don't have to fake it with me. I know you're not exactly glad to see me, especially after how I left."

"Well, Carla, I—"

"Shh. Please let me finish," she replied as she placed a single finger on his lips. Just feeling her touch again melted his heart, but he couldn't allow his emotions to get in the way, not now, not ever. DeTroyt very politely moved her hand.

Carla didn't like rejection and had a hard time hiding it, so she followed accordingly. "I'm sorry. Listen, I'm only in town for a few days on business and my sister told me what happened, you know, the accident and all and what they were doing for you here at the church. So I figured I should at least face you after all these years." She paused and waited for a response, but he didn't offer one. "DeTroyt, I know this hasn't been easy for you and I don't want to hurt you anymore than I have—"

"Carla," he cut in. "This is neither the time nor the place to discuss this."

"I understand that, but I just wanted to—" Carla started to explain, but DeTroyt cut in again.

"Why are you still talking?" DeTroyt asked. "I said this is *not* the time or place to have this discussion." He realized he was speaking out of anger and quickly apologized. "Look, I'm sorry. Here, this is my number at home," he said as he handed her a card like the one he handed to LaShae. "Call me later and we'll talk then. I have to go find Vicki."

"That's who I want to talk to you about."

"Who? My daughter?" he asked in amazement.

Carla stood there for a moment, knowing what he was getting at. "No, Troy. *Our* daughter."

"What? What do you mean *our* daughter? No, no, no. See, you gave up those rights when you shipped her to my grandmother's house with a note attached. I didn't know where you were, how to find you, or how you were doing. Goodness, Carla, I didn't even know that you were pregnant!" Troy realized that his voice was carrying, so he pulled her out into the foyer of the church to continue their conversation. "I've been raising her for eleven years, and I am not about to let you just waltz back into our lives. No, Carla! End of discussion! Goodnight!" he exclaimed, making arm movements as if he were calling a safe play at a baseball game. With that, he turned and headed back into the church where his guests were waiting for him.

"DeTroyt, honey, wait! Please hear me out."

But it was too late. DeTroyt had shut the door to the foyer, closing the distance between himself and Carla.

It took everything in him to keep from turning around and running after her. Just seeing her again made him weak in the knees, even after all of these years.

"Daddy! Hi! What took you so long? I've been looking for you. I need to tell you about this lady I met a little while ago."

"What lady?" DeTroyt knew very well who she meant.

Vicki shrugged. "I don't know. She said she was an old friend of yours, and she was looking for you."

They started on their way to the dining hall. "Did she have a name?"

To look at his daughter and see her mother was so painful. They were so much alike, starting from the long coal, black hair to the soles of their feet. DeTroyt wondered why Carla would come back now after all these years. Did she want to take her back with her to Ohio?

"Yeah," she answered while munching on grapes. "She had a name. It was Carla. She really wanted to see you. Hey, there she is right there."

Turning in the direction Vicki was pointing, DeTroyt saw Carla re-enter the room.

"She's very pretty, Daddy. Why is she looking so hard to find you?" she asked with a touch of humor.

"I promise I'll explain later, but right now I have to…"

"Come on, son, we set this night aside just for you," said Pastor Simms. "We can't start the festivities without the main attraction," he continued, placing his arms on DeTroyt's shoulder.

"Okay, Pastor. I'll be right there. Just let me take care of something right quick," he said looking in Carla's direction.

Pastor Simms let out a sigh. "Alright, but make it quick. You know you can't keep us waiting too long with a bunch of food around." With that, he smiled and turned to go back to his seat at the table in the dining hall.

"Yes, sir," he said. "Now back to you," he stated, turning to Vicki. "I'll talk to you a little later, okay? I promise. Now, run along to the dining hall. I'll be there in a minute."

"Okay, Daddy," said Vicki. She then motioned for DeTroyt to lean down. As soon as he did, she kissed him on the cheek. "You promised," she said as she returned to the dining area.

DeTroyt, turning in Carla's direction, practically ran right into her. Their faces were inches apart, and DeTroyt quickly stepped back.

"I see you got rid of her just in time, huh?"

"Carla, why are you still here? I gave you my number to call me later, so why won't you do that? I do not want her to find out about you like this. Not here."

"Well, when are you going to tell her about me, D? When she turns 21 and has nothing to say to me? I can't leave without her knowing, Troy!" Carla said, growing impatient.

"You shouldn't have spoken to her without my consent."

"Without *your* consent? The child doesn't even know who I am, and I guess you made sure of that!"

"Yeah, you're right. I made sure that she never saw a picture or even spoke with anyone related to you because of moments like these. We will continue this later, Carla. Goodbye."

Instead of walking toward the foyer door, Carla walked past him and sat down on one of the pews. He followed but remained standing. She tried holding the tears back for as long as she could, but the pain of not being able to communicate with Vicki, even through her mistakes, was just too much. "Regardless of what I did, I still have a right to see her. I am still her mother…"

"The mother who left her on my grandmother's porch in a bassinet with a note attached," he continued. "To me, that meant you didn't want to have anything to do with her or me."

Standing, she asked, "Are you ever going to let that go, DeTroyt?"

"No!"

"Why?"

"Why? You don't get it, do you?" His voice was more stern than before, which startled Carla a little. "Carla, out of the eleven years of your absence, how many times have we heard from you? None. And now you think because everything is okay with you that you can come into our lives again like nothing happened?"

"I didn't have a choice."

"Yes, you did. You had me! You could have come to me, Carla, but you didn't."

Carla wanted to defend herself but decided against it. She could see how upset DeTroyt was getting, so she left it alone… at least for now.

"Look, there are people waiting for me in the next room, and I don't want to ruin this for them. You can either join us or leave us."

With that said, Carla decided to leave. She did not want to cause any more damage by speaking with Vicki right now.

As she approached the door, she turned to face DeTroyt. "This is not over." She then left the building.

DeTroyt waited to see if she was going to return before joining the others, but she did not.

Before joining the others, he said a quick prayer of repentance for his thoughts.

"I do apologize for my tardiness. I had something to take care of," he announced, sounding very apologetic.

"Well, Bro Maning," started Deacon Martin, who was, because of his tenure, the most highly respected deacon at the church. "That was some stunt you pulled, risking your life to save the life of another. What was her name again? LaTrice?"

DeTroyt gave a smirk to his effort before replying to him. "Well,

Deacon Martin, it's actually LaShae and I must say that God was with me… with us, the entire time. I really couldn't have done it without His help," he exclaimed, pointing his index finger upwards. "LaShae is a beautiful young lady, and I just appreciate the fact that I was obedient."

"Alright then!" yelled someone in the corner. "Let's eat!"

From then on, DeTroyt's night went well. There was lots of food, friends, and fellowship… not to mention a little Word going on.

Chapter Eight

Carla

THE PLOT

Outside of the church walls, Carla placed a phone call.

"Yes, I'm here," she answered. She listened and answered again.

"No! He won't budge. I knew he wouldn't. He wouldn't even allow me to speak to her. He kept sending her away every time I came near. I don't know what I'm gonna do."

She listened again.

"She has no clue of who I am. He hasn't even shown her a picture of me, let alone told her anything about me. He probably told her that I was dead for all I know. He gave me his number, as if I didn't have it already, to call him later. They were giving him a surprise dinner for being a hero to some chick he saved in a car accident."

She listened again.

"Yeah, beats me. These people really love him though and I truly understand why. He's a good man, stubborn, but good and the things that he said to me about me were hurtful but true."

She listened.

"No, I'm not beating myself up, just stating facts. He's been so good to Vicki; she's a beautiful young girl. She has my hair, my complexion, but his eyes and nose, and a combination of both our builds. I'll be glad when you can meet her, Aaron."

Aaron Saltwater, a defense attorney and Carla's husband, had been standing by her since he first learned of Vicki and Carla's decision to finally meet the little girl. This had not been an easy journey for his wife of nine years. Carla had struggled with the fact that she had to give her daughter up or suffer the consequences that followed, so she did. Carla returned to her hometown and left Vicki on DeTroyt grandmother's porch with a note that read:

DeTroyt,

I am so sorry that you have to find out this way, but this is your daughter, Vicki. OUR daughter. Please take care of her, as I cannot.

I pray that you can and will understand my plea. She's beautiful, D. She has your eyes and nose. Please find it in your heart to forgive me.

Love always,
Carla

Carla kept a copy of the note as a reminder of what she had to do if she ever decided to see Vicki again.

When she and Aaron first met on her first day at OSU, he was very sweet and polite. Not quite her type, nor was he DeTroyt, but she was definitely drawn to him. It took a little bit for her to warm up to him, but when she finally did, finally gave her all to him, there was no turning back. Carla told Aaron everything and yet he still chose to love her, and they've been together ever since.

"If she's anything like her mother, I'm sure I will love her," Aaron replied.

Carla smiled. "Yes, you will. I love you, Aaron. I'll be home in a few days."

"I love you too, honey," Aaron replied. "Talk with you soon."

They hung up and Carla proceeded to her car. Little did she know, her entire conversation fell on open ears.

Watching Carla get into her car, Erica emerged from the shadows.

"So you're the little brat's long-lost dead mother, huh?" she asked to no one in particular. "I'm anxious to see where this leads."

With this bit of information, she had something to work with. "So Vicki doesn't know her mother is actually alive."

Erica had to smile to herself. She'll use that information when the time is right.

With that, she opened the church doors and joined the celebration.

Chapter Nine

Keven-n-MyChele

YOU DID, WHAT???!!!

"MyChele, how could you?" Keven asked furiously. "You know—"

"Shae kicked me out before I could finish. She believes you were with me on those days instead."

Keven stopped pacing long enough to look at her in astonishment. "With you? I know you lying! She didn't think that! I can't even believe that one."

"Hey, what does that supposed to mean?" she asked, striking a pose like a diva girl.

"You know what I mean. Geez! That's beside the point, Chele. You have opened up a door that was shut and sealed long ago," he said, pacing the floor. "I've got to straighten this out!" Angry that he even confided in her, he sat down at his dining room table and put his head down to keep from looking at her.

Mychele sat on the stool next to him. "Keven, you know you can trust me with anything. She told me what went down between you two and started reminiscing about your relationship." She paused for a minute to give him time to respond, but got nothing. "Kev, Shae is so hurt right now. She cries at the mention of your name. So you know, when she cries, I cry and I just get caught up," she explained, throwing her hands up. "I never meant to even touch that part of your past, man. I am so, so sorry. I never meant to—

"How could I be so stupid?" he asked lifting his head to face MyChele. She could see the hurt in his eyes and hear the pain in his voice. "One for leaving LaShae and two for trusting you. I really love her, MyChele and I–I just can't get it right. My baby has done nothing to make me act the way that I did. I was trying to be hard and cover up my mess, but she didn't deserve to be treated like that. I remember the things that I did to her, especially when she was pregnant with Kaleb."

Forgetting the I love yous and what have yous, something he said stuck out with her. MyChele gave Keven a look that would cut him in half had her eyes been knives. She had to know.

"But you don't even believe that he's your son."

"Chele, Kaleb *is* my son. I've *always* known that, but back then, I wanted to believe that she cheated on me so that I wouldn't feel so guilty about messing up on her. So I lied to everyone about the baby and now I can't see him at all. What can I do now? Shae hates me and Kaleb doesn't even know me. I've hurt them so badly, MyChele. I've hurt them so much. I've got to make this right again," he said through tears.

MyChele put her hand on his shoulder to try and console him, but he pushed it away.

"She almost died and guess who gets to be by her side? Some stranger! Chele, I should've been by her side, not him!" Keven pushed away from the table and began to pace the floor as the phone rang. Apparently, not hearing it over his anger, he continued, "Had I not broken up with her, none of this probably wouldn't have happened, ya know?"

Keven finally heard the phone over the commotion and motioned for MyChele to answer it. She was hesitant, but she did.

"Hello?"

There was no answer.

"Hel-lo," she said, a second time.

"MyChele?" a familiar voice came.

"Shae?" MyChele did not know what to think, say, or do. On the other end of this line sat the person that was under the impression her best friend slept with her boyfriend. This, of course, did not look good at all.

"What are you doing over there?" she asked.

In the midst of Mychele trying to explain, Keven rushed over and grabbed the phone from her. "Shae, I can explain."

"You know? Don't bother! You two have a happy life!"

Click.

"Shae! Shae wait!" Keven tried to call her back several times, but each call went straight to voicemail. "I'm going over there."

With that, he grabbed his keys and rushed out the door. MyChele followed closely. He jumped in the driver seat of his SUV. MyChele opened the passenger side and began to get in.

"Where are you going?"

"Well, with you, Keven. You know, for assistance."

"Oh, hell no," he replied. "You've assisted enough. You're the reason why I'm in this mess now. Get out!" He then gave her a slight nudge out of the truck.

She did what he asked and closed the door. She turned to him and asked, "So what am I supposed to do?"

"Isn't that your car over there?" he asked, pointing at the black BMW in the driveway.

"Yes," she replied.

"Well, get in it and go home. Shae and I really need to be alone right now," he replied as he backed out of the driveway.

Mychele looked on as Keven drove away. "This isn't the end, pretty boy," she promised. Then she got into her car and left.

Chapter Ten

La Shae

REALLY... FORGIVE YOU?

LaShae had gone back to her house a little after she had woken up. She felt that she could rest better in her own bed, that was until she called Keven. She called to get some things off of her chest.

Ha! The nerve of her, answering his phone like she lives there. Well, maybe she does. You know, what? They deserve each other. Bunch of lowlifes. Who in the...?

"Mommy, may I have some water?" Kaleb asked in a sleepy voice. "I'm *really* thirsty."

LaShae wiped her face before turning around to face him. "Yes, baby. Let's go get you some water."

As they started down the narrow hallway toward the kitchen, Kaleb turned to say, "Come on skip with me, Mommy."

"Baby, Mommy's not really in the skipping mood right now."

Kaleb stopped dead in his tracks, making LaShae lose her balance a little.

"Hey bud, what's the matter"? LaShae asked as she knelt down beside him.

Pouting he replied, "You won't skip with me"

"Oh, honey," she replied, hugging him real tight. "I'm sorry, but Mommy just... " LaShae paused mid-sentence. *What the heck?* she thought. She can do this one little thing for him. "You know what?" she asked with a big grin on her face.

"What?" Kaleb responded still with the pouty face.

"Let's skip, okay?"

His eyes lit up at the suggestion. "Okay."

"That's my boy. Let's go." They skipped about three times and were in the kitchen. Even though it was a short distance, considering they had walked the majority of the way, he was so happy. *Why should I make him suffer for something his father did?*

She watched Kaleb drink his water and skip to the bathroom to do his nightly bathroom routine before returning to bed. On their way back to his bedroom, there was a knock at the door. LaShae, knowing she was not expecting anyone, cautiously went to answer it. She left Kaleb in the hallway away from the door. She opened the door to see Keven standing there and immediately tried to close it; however, he stuck his foot in the door, jamming it from closing.

"Who is it, Mommy?" Kaleb asked from down the hall.

Still having eye contact with Keven, she answered, "Nobody, baby. Absolutely nobody. Go to your room, sweetheart. I'll be there in a minute."

He grudgingly went, looking back at his mom every so often with those sad puppy dog eyes. She left Keven standing on the opposite side of the door long enough to take care of her son.

Once Kaleb was settled, she returned to the front door where, unfortunately, Keven was still waiting. With no remorse, she lit into him like the fourth of July. "What the hell are you doing here? You are not welcome in my home anymore." With a hint of jealousy, she added, "I thought you'd be having a blast with *your girl* right about now."

"I truly deserve that," he stated matter of factly. "May I please come in?"

Even though she left a handprint on the side of his face, there was not an ounce of anger in his voice. LaShae was confused. She had never known him to let an opportunity for a fight pass him by.

After standing there for a minute and realizing that he wasn't going to leave, she stepped aside to let him in. Out of the eight years of their relationship, Keven never expressed this type of calmness during a confrontation, especially after being hit. In fact, when she opened the door, his eyes were red and puffy. Had he been crying? If so, for what reason?

"What do you want, Keven Mitchell?" LaShae asked, growing impatient.

"I want you to listen to *me* for a change," he answered in the same tone he had when he asked to come in.

"Listen to you? Listen to you? I think the last time that I *listened to you*, I was hospitalized. You've made your point quite clearly. Therefore, you don't have anything to say that I would want to *listen* to." With that, she went toward the door and opened it, letting Keven know that his presence was no longer welcomed. "Now get out."

Keven walked toward the door, but instead of going out of it as she had hoped, grabbed her free hand and gently closed the door with his other hand. "Please Shae, come sit down with me please." He led her over to the couch and sat down. LaShae slid as far away as she could.

"Baby, this is very important. Please hear me out," Keven stated. His voice was so soft and quiet, so LaShae knew that he must be serious. Even though she didn't want to hear anything that he had to say, let alone be in his presence, she stayed quiet.

Shae, no matter what he says, do not go soft, girl. Keep your guards up and you'll be okay.

"LaShae," Keven started as he faced her, fumbling nervously with his keys.

"What?" she snapped.

"Listen," he started. "First of all, please don't be upset with MyChele. When you called me, I asked Chele to answer the phone, not to get you angry or have you think that something was going on between us because there's not and there never was. She came over to tell me what you all talked about. I didn't know it was you on the other end, I swear!"

Keven slid a little closer to her to fill the gap between them. Not too close that she would pull away, but close enough to make full and complete eye contact.

"Shae, I know that I've done some dirt in this relationship. Some things you know about and others that don't even matter, but to hear those things first hand really made me realize how stupid and selfish I was. Baby, you were the last person that I ever wanted to hurt. You mean the world to me. I really want to make this right with you *and* Kaleb. I've never stopped believing he was my son. I just wasn't ready—"

"Oh and I was?"

"I know you weren't, and I'm sorry. I should have been a little more careful in that department." There was a slight pause before he continued. "I'm also sorry for not being there for you when Kaleb was born. I should have been a man about it. I'm sorry for not being around to see him grow up into the little man that he is now. I mean, I really missed out on a very important part of his life… of our life."

He paused and LaShae could see the tears welling up in his eyes. She quickly turned away. She couldn't afford to watch him cry because it hurt too much. However, she wished for him to be hurt for everything he had ever done to her and Kaleb.

Slowly, as if in a trance, he continued, "Shae, we've known each other since the seventh grade and I've loved no one but you since then. I'm embarrassed to say that I never knew how much I love you until I thought that I had lost you. I know the reason behind the way I had acted with you. I was afraid—"

"Afraid of what, Keven?"

"Afraid of being hurt. Even when I saw that you poured your entire heart out to me, I figured I would protect myself and surround myself with other people, females to be exact. I know now that I was selfish and I found out in the end that it not only hurt me, but my family as well."

"Your family? What does your mama and them have to do with this?" she asked, not really buying into his little speech.

He had to let out a chuckle before he responded. "Not them, you and Kaleb. *You* are my family." His voice began to get shaky. "LaShae, I want to be able to see my son. I'm ready to take that responsibility now."

So much for keeping my guards up and my mouth shut. "What?" LaShae was floored. "So you expect me to drag Kaleb into this mess of a relationship only to be devastated in the end? Have you lost your mind? It's one thing to have me suffer with whether or not I'm gonna see you today or tomorrow or if or when you're gonna call or worry about when you're going to decide to end our relationship. I cannot and will not allow you to hurt my baby that way." She was now an emotional wreck, pacing the floor in front of the television which she had turned on to camouflage their talking. "That little boy deserves so much better than you and you know it," she stated, not able to hold back the tears any longer.

"Now wait a minute—" Keven said defensively.

"No, *you* wait a minute," she cut in, now standing in front of Keven. "You've been a father for five years and you've just realized it? If Chele and I had not had that conversation to begin with, you wouldn't be here now. You know why? Because you wouldn't feel guilty about it. Your ego got crushed and now you think you can waltz in here, cry a few tears, and we're supposed to let you back into our lives and pretend that nothing is wrong? Well, a lot is wrong so you can really just get out!"

"Baby, wait," he said, reaching for her hand as she walked toward the door.

Jerking away, she continued on her journey to escort Keven out the door.

"LaShae, please listen to me. I love you with all my heart, and I always have. You've got to believe me."

"Believe? I'll tell you what I believe. I believe you feel guilty about cheating on me, denying your child, accusing me of sleeping around, and not to mention abusing me mentally and emotionally—"

All of a sudden, he kissed her.

Oh, my God! Okay, I've gotta kick him out! He has to leave now! I don't care how much I love him, this cannot go any further.

LaShae was finally able to pull away, but there was something in his eyes that distracted her. It was a look that she'd never seen before. A twinkle of some sort! The two stood there, lost in each other's eyes for what seemed like eternity. LaShae felt so confused, but she couldn't let him see her break. Looking into his eyes, she saw the truth, but her head and heart were not in agreement right now. She felt him getting closer to her and even though she tried to pull away, his grip was too tight.

"Marry me, Shae."

She was so caught off guard she stumbled for words. "Marry… what? For what? So that you can keep tabs on me and Kaleb? Get over your guilt, Keven! Get out of my house, and while you're at it, go to hell!" she said through gritted teeth.

Keven would not take no for an answer no matter what LaShae did or said to him.

"LaShae, I love you and I meant everything I said to you tonight. I want to be a part of my son's life. I want to spend the rest of my life with you… with both of you." He placed a hand under her chin and lifted her face to his. "Shae, I know that I've messed up in the past, but there's nothing I can do to change that. I am willing to start over… if you will have me."

With that, he got down on one knee and pulled out the most

beautiful ring she had ever seen. "LaShae Moniiq Wilson, will you marry me?"

LaShae was so busy looking at the ring, she never noticed the tears that were being shared between the both of them.

The next day was very bright for LaShae. She woke up on cloud nine. Though she wanted Keven to spend the night, she felt it was best for him to go home to his own place.

Yes! We are officially engaged, finally! she thought, but at the same time, she had her qualms about it.

LaShae stood in front of her bathroom mirror and for the first time, really took a hard look at herself. "What did I do?!"

Chapter Eleven

LaShae & DeTroyt

TWO MONTHS LATER (THE RUMOR)

"Good afternoon. Thank you for calling Gibson's Jewelry and Design, this is Zhandra. How may I help you?"

"Zhandra, this is Shae. Is my m—"

"Oh, hey girl!" Zhandra interrupted. "How are you feeling? Are you getting much rest? Are you excited? Ooo girl, I would be. I'm more excited than you are and I'm not even expect—"

"Expecting? Zhan, what are you babbling about? And what truck hit you this morning on your way to work?" LaShae was still unsure as to what Zhan was talking about.

"Mhmm, it wasn't the same truck that hit you two months ago, that's for sure," Zhandra answered.

Zhandra Reed was one of Jasmyn's new employees. She was hired to assist Jake with his daily duties and to pick up the slack when he was not there. Needless to say, he trained her well. She gossiped just as much as he did.

"What?" LaShae was very confused at this point and wanted Zhandra to spit out whatever it was she was getting at.

Finally frustrated because LaShae wasn't giving her the answer she wanted, she took a big sigh and asked, "Aren't you expecting his baby?"

"Whoa, whoa, whoa. Slow down girl! What baby and who's the daddy?" she asked, now sitting up in her bed. She decided to take the day off to rest. Since the accident, she's been having pains here and there that disabled her from sitting or standing for long periods of time. That was all she would need to hear, so LaShae kept that part to herself.

"DeTroyt's baby!" Zhandra said with enthusiasm.

LaShae, stunned by this accusation, tried to make herself wake up from this nightmare. Well, at least she was hoping that she was dreaming.

Zhandra had no idea that LaShae had strong feelings for DeTroyt and this was a very cruel joke. "Oh my God! Where did you hear that?"

Smirking, Zhandra replied, "A reliable source."

LaShae, now shouting through the receiver, demanded, "Girl, stop playing with me. Now tell me who told you that!"

"I got a whiff of it in the lounge here," Zhandra answered. "I don't know where it originated from. You know I'm still new here, so I don't know everyone by name. I just heard your name and his name in the same sentence, so I pretended to read a magazine and that is what came out of the conversation. Not too reliable, huh? Shae, I'm so sorry. I didn't mean to upset you like this." The enthusiasm had left Zhandra's voice and was replaced with embarrassment.

"Well, from now on Zhandra, if you want to make sure, please come to me first, okay?" LaShae began explaining. "I cannot afford for my reputation nor DeTroyt's to get ruined, especially when we're not even a unit."

"You're not?" Zhan asked in surprise. "Oh, no."

"What now?" Shae asked, rolling her eyes toward the ceiling. "Your reliable source again?"

"Well…" Zhandra started.oh well let's

Frustrated, Shae just dropped the whole thing. "You know what? I don't even want to know. Is my mother available?"

"Sure, just a moment." While Zhandra was transferring LaShae to Jasmyn's line, her other line beeped.

Oh hurry up, Mama. Answer the phone. After the third ring, Jasmyn's voicemail came on, but instead of leaving a message, she clicked over to the other line. "Hello?"

"Shae?" started the voice on the other end.

"Mama, I just tried to call you but I got your voicemail." She waited for a response but didn't get one. "Mama, what's wrong? Where are you?"

Jasmyn was silent for what seemed like half an hour before responding. "LaShae, we need to talk face to face. Meet me at Monzo's diner across the street from my office building in about half an hour. Bring an overnight bag."

"An overnight bag? Mama, what's going on?"

"Just do it! Please," Jasmyn said with a little frustration in her voice.

LaShae was really starting to worry about her mother. "Alright, Mama. I'll come, but what have I don–" All she heard was a click from the other end. Jasmyn hung up before LaShae could get the question out. *What is going on? I should have gone to work.*

After dragging herself out of bed to get ready to face whatever was wrong with her mother, the telephone rang as soon as she opened up the door to leave. She decided not to answer it until she heard DeTroyts' voice on the answering machine.

She raced to the phone and almost dropped her crystal glass that she always took with her on trips. Luckily, it dropped on the couch.

"Hello? Hello? DeTroyt?" she answered, trying to catch him before he hung up the phone.

"LaShae? What is going on?" she finally heard him say.

"I don't know what—"

"Don't play innocent with me, young lady!" he snapped.

"What?"

"What's with all the rumors, Shae?" he questioned. His voice sounded more firm with her than usual. "I thought I could trust you! We've become very close over the past couple of months and within that time, you've found out more things about me than I've told people in all my life. Just because I'm engaged doesn't give you the right to ruin my reputation, not to mention put a question of doubt in my fiancée's head."

"Engaged? Fiancée? You told me everything, but *that*!" she said dumbfounded. "That's beside the point right now. What are you talking about? Don't say that I know because I don't!"

Frustrated now, he raised his voice. "The rumors, Shae! You know! The one about you being pregnant with my child!"

She hung her head shaking it in disbelief. Before responding, she let out a deep sigh. "Oh, those rumors."

"Oh? What do you mean, '*Oh*?' Is that all you can say? Do you know what you've done to my reputation, not to mention my future with Erica?" DeTroyt was about to hang up the phone, but he must've heard her sniffling. "What are you crying for? I'm the one that should be crying."

LaShae tried to catch her breath between sobs. Finally, she was able to speak. "All you're thinking about is yourself! What about me, DeTroyt? My name was put out there too. I have a reputation to protect just like you do. Just because I'm not partially attached to someone like you are it makes it okay for my name to be disgraced, right? I don't know where this came from or even why it got started." LaShae sniffed again before continuing. "You should know me by now, D. I would never cause pain or embarrassment to you even if you weren't in the church. That's just wrong."

There was brief silence on the other end. "What are you saying? That you didn't have anything to do with this?"

"No, I didn't! How could you ask me something like that? I just found out about it a few minutes ago when I called my mother at work. Her receptionist asked me about it."

DeTroyt had calmed down and his voice was a little more sympathetic toward her. He was finally relieved to know that LaShae had nothing to do with this mess.

Still sniffing and sobbing, LaShae flopped down on the couch. Her back was beginning to hurt again from standing for just that short period of time. "I think that's why my mother is so angry with me. She asked me to pack some clothes and meet her at Monzo's Diner across from her office building. I guess we were going somewhere."

DeTroyt let out a soft, "Oh."

"DeTroyt, I don't know where this came from or why it even exists. I'm sorry that you're in the middle of this… this… mess. You know I would never hurt you like that. You mean too much to me. Your friendship means too much to me."

There was silence on the other end of the phone. DeTroyt's mind replayed the beginning of their conversation until now. "I know you wouldn't," he finally said. "I don't even know why I thought that you would or could do something like this to me. Look Shae, I'm really, really sorry about all of this. I know I shouldn't have come at you like that. Could you find it in your heart to forgive me, please?" DeTroyt was very sincere in his asking, and LaShae felt deeply that he meant it.

Smiling, she answered, "Yes, my heart forgives you. In the meantime, I would appreciate it if you wouldn't give it a cardiac arrest."

A smile came across DeTroyts' lips that made his voice sound a little cheerier.

"You have my word," he promised.

Getting her mind ready to face another head on collision with her mother, LaShae made ready to get off the phone. "Well, Mr. Maning, I have to go now before my mother shows up on my doorstep." Just as she finished her statement, her doorbell rang. "Well, too late."

"We need to find out where this rumor originated from, but in the meantime, I'll keep your mother in my prayers for your sake. Call me later, okay?"

"Okay! But if I want to live to see later, I'd better open this door. Bye!"

After hanging up the phone, LaShae rushed to the door only to find MyChele standing there. She froze in her steps. *What is she doing here?*

"Did you lose something?" LaShae asked, not too moved to see her.

She stood there for a minute before answering. "Is it true?"

"Is what true?" LaShae asked, knowing full well what MyChele was talking about. LaShae had already gathered her belongings *again* while racing to the door. All she could do was stare in dismay.

"You know exactly what I'm talking about. You being pregnant! How could you do that to Keven? I thought he meant something to you." MyChele seemed a little jealous mixed in with a bit of ticked-off.

"Chele, I am not going to go through this with you, not now." LaShae thought about it again. "Why should what I do to Keven matter to you anyway? You didn't think about what *you* did to me nor our friendship! It's not like you care or anything. You're just being nosy, and that *my friend*, I don't need," LaShae replied, shifting her belongings in her arms as well as her weight to balance out the load.

The look on Mychele's face was as guilty as a cat caught stealing fish from a garbage can. She tried to cover her deceit, but was unable to. "I do care!" she finally responded. "Just because we are not speaking doesn't mean that I don't care about what happens to you. We've been best friends since seventh grade, Shae. No matter how you look at it, you are always going to be just that."

"Really." LaShae's response was more of a statement than a question. "Well, my definition of a 'best friend' is someone who is always there for you no matter what. Someone who will love you for you and be that shoulder to cry on. Not someone who sleeps with their best friend's boyfriend and pretends that everything is okay." With that, LaShae closed her front door and brushed past Chele as if she was not even there.

"LaShae, wait." She reached out to try and grab LaShae's arm as she passed.

"This conversation is over. Now leave," LaShae said between gritted teeth. LaShae looked on as MyChele got in her car and started the engine. Slowly, MyChele made her way to her car and out of the driveway. Tears welled up in LaShae's eyes as she reminisced about all of the good times they shared and the tears they cried together. She just had to go and sleep with her boyfriend. *The nerve of her to come to my house*, LaShae thought as she backed out of the driveway.

Chapter Twelve

Jasmyn & LaShae

THE VISITOR @ THE DINER

Jasmyn was growing impatient. It was nearly four o'clock and LaShae had not shown up yet. Every now and then, her waitress would come by and ask her if she needed anything.

"No, sweetie. Thank you," she replied as politely as she could.

The young lady left Jasmyn's table and began waiting on her other customers.

The politeness didn't last for long. Jasmyn looked up to see LaShae enter the diner a half an hour late.

"Hi, Mama. I'm so sorry I'm late but—"

She gave LaShae a *look* before saying anything. "LaShae Moniiq Wilson, sit down!"

LaShae has never seen her mother act this way. Her hands were shaking and her eyes were red and swollen as though she'd been crying for days.

"Mama, what's wrong? Why are you acting like this?" LaShae reached for her mother's hand, but Jasmyn pulled back as though LaShae had some sort of disease.

"Mama, would you talk to me?" LaShae exclaimed as quietly as she could without making a scene. "What is wrong with you? What have I done?" LaShae was surprised at how much her voice cracked as she tried to swallow the hard lump in her throat. She tried to hold her tears back, but one escaped already and rolled down her cheek.

Jasmyn threw a piece of paper onto the table. It was folded in three parts like a business letter.

"This is what's wrong with me, LaShae. How could you do this to, not only me, but yourself? I thought you wanted to finish school and—"

"Pregnancy?" LaShae exclaimed. "Positive? What? Mama, where did you get this… and with my name on it?" she managed to ask. There was something going on, and she was going to find out what it was and who was behind it.

Raising her eyebrows, she asked, "So you deny it?"

"There's nothing to deny because it's not true. How dare you not trust me? I'm outta here!" LaShae got up from the table and was about to walk off when she felt a tight grip on her forearm.

"Don't you ever walk away from me, young lady!" hissed

Jasmyn. "I'm not finished with you yet." She slowly released her arm and continued. "You wait outside until I pay for this check, and we'll go somewhere else where we can talk more openly about this."

"Mother, we have nothing more to discuss." Her sassiness earned another angry look from her mother, but this time it didn't matter. With that, LaShae snatched away and stormed out of the diner. Tears streaming from her eyes, she jumped in her car and was about to start the engine when the passenger side door opened, startling her. Assuming it was Jasmyn, immediately, she said, "This conversation is over, Mother."

"Nah, sweet cakes, it's just beginning," came the familiar voice.

LaShae regretfully turned only to see the one person she thought could never bother her again. That face, those eyes, even that sheepish grin chilled her very soul. Breathless, she couldn't say anything. Suddenly, LaShae felt sick to her stomach. *Stephon Knight is still alive, but how did he find me?*

"So, I see you've been doing well for yourself. How nice, Peaches," Stephon complimented.

Stephon always had a way of talking to her, even when they first met 10 years ago in that dark alley when LaShae was only 15 years old. It was a very cold night and LaShae had run away from home because her stepfather was molesting her every chance he got. Because she was an only child, there was really no one that she could talk to, not her best friend Mychele and especially not her mother. Stephon seemed so nice and gentle and he made LaShae feel like a queen. Even though he wasn't that much older than her, he knew how to treat a lady or... so it seems. He took her in and took care of her until she was strong enough to start taking care of herself which didn't take very long to do. He told her that he could help her find a good job, making more money than she has ever seen in her whole life. LaShae went with it, and Stephon introduced her to prostitution and pole dancing. That was the one thing she was trying to avoid by running away from home, but because he threatened to hurt her if she didn't agree to his terms, she gave in. LaShae (Stephon nicknamed her "Peaches," when she worked for him) couldn't see no way out of it in the beginning. Soon, there were television reports of her being missing and her mother pleading for her to come back home.

One night, while working at her post, which was four hours away from her parents' home, a client came in and she performed her usual lap dance and then led him back to her room where she did the rest of her job. Before she could get the door locked, the mysterious gentleman swung her around and introduced himself as an undercover agent who had come to take her out of that dump. He explained to her that Jasmyn hired him to find her by any means necessary. When LaShae heard the news, she jumped up and hugged him with all her might. The agent quickly pushed her away and explained to her that they didn't have much time and for her to put on some clothes and grab whatever she could of her things and get out.

Lucky for LaShae, her window didn't have bars on it, unlike the other girls' windows. She guessed that was because Stephon had grown to trust her so much that he didn't feel like he had to put them on her windows. That night was the best night that LaShae has ever had working for Stephon.

"How did you find me?" she asked, without even so much as a blink. LaShae tried to stare a hole into his eye socket.

"Now, now, Peaches, you know I have my connections and I can't reveal my sources," he said, revealing the smile that drew her in at the age of 15. Instead of appealing to her, it just made her angry.

Her veins began to pop out the angrier she got. She was ready to attack, but for the moment, she held her peace. "What do you want?" she asked through gritted teeth.

"Ya know, Peaches, seven years is a long time to be away from someone, especially me. Let's say we pick up from where we left off, huh?" He touched her face with his cold and rough hands.

Pulling away with disgust, she asked yet again, "What do you want?"

"Do as you're told and no one gets hurt."

"Who the hell are you to make threats? Have you forgotten whom you're talking to? Don't you remember what happened the last time you threatened me?"

Her thoughts were cut real short when she realized there was a very sharp object pressing against her neck. *A knife! Oh my God, a knife! Okay, Shae, stay calm. Don't make any sudden moves. Breathe, babygirl! Breathe!*

"What are you—" she tried to ask, but the point got sharper.

"Shut up, LaShae! See, I'm trying to do this without force, but your mouth is gonna get you into a lot of trouble. If you cooperate with me, then I won't hurt you or Kaleb. There is something that has to be done and you *will* help me do it! Do you understand me?"

Silence filled the air.

"Do you understand me, Peaches? I don't want to hurt you."

Reluctantly, she answered. "Yes, I understand. What is this about?"

"You know what this is about. I want you to come back to Philly with me. I need some more girls, and you've been getting a lot of requests. That's bad for my business if I can't deliver what my clients want. You don't want me to lose any money now, do you? I lost enough when you ran away from me and thought you got away. I've always known where you were and what you were doing. You'll never be able to escape me." He had a smirk on his face as if he knew everything about her.

"I don't do that anymore, and I will never go anywhere with you again. I was only 15! You ruined my life! Wasn't that enough?"

"Don't play saint with me, little girl. You know that you will always be a whore no matter how much you say you're not." He leaned over a little closer to her face, and he still held the knife at her throat.

"I'm not a whore!" she said through gritted teeth.

"Remember your welcome home party? You never knew I was there. It kind of bothered me that you didn't notice me, you know, with us being so close and all. You and your little friend, MyChele, were too busy drooling over Mr. Maning to even notice."

"What do you mean you were there? My mother would never invite you into her home. She hates you and so do I!" At this point, she didn't care if he had two knives at her throat. He was really getting on her nerves.

"Ta-ta-ta. You know you're not supposed to hate. It's in the B-I-B-L-E. Didn't your *church* friend teach you anything?"

"Don't you dare bring the Bible into this mess. You are by no means a saint! You sell teenage girls like they're nothing. I'm glad I got away."

He moved the knife from her neck and pressed it into her side instead. She could feel something trickle down her side. "Ow, you're hurting me. Let me go!" she demanded.

He pulled the knife from her side and sat back in the seat and began to laugh. "You know, Peaches, I could really hurt you if I wanted to but I'm gonna let you go right now because I want you to witness the horror that I will bring upon your little friends and family. But I will be getting in touch with you and if you mention this conversation to anyone, it's over for you and Kaleb."

And just like that, Stephon was gone. He'd slipped out of the car just as quickly as he'd slipped into the car and disappeared into a dark alley.

LaShae was speechless.

Okay, first I'm fighting with DeTroyt about some rumor, then my mama, and now this creep who I thought was locked away in my past came back?

"I don't get it! I just don't get it!"

No sooner than she got those words out, Jasmyn approached and got into the passenger side. She sat in the car for at least half an hour before pulling off. All the while, LaShae was trying to piece this mysterious puzzle together.

LaShae made it back to her house and was in the bathroom nursing her wound. Hearing the sound of her cell phone chirping made her jump. She answered with hesitation. "Hel-lo?"

"LaShae?"

"Yes?"

"Hey, this is DeTroyt. Are you okay? You sound a bit disturbed."

There was nothing that she could say to hide her emotions, so she didn't answer his question. "What's up?" she asked instead, trying to be as enthused as possible without giving her true feelings away.

"I was calling to see how things went with Jasmyn. You don't sound as though they went well at all."

Again, hesitating to say anything, she said, "Well, things got a bit out of hand. She told me to wait for her in my car and she would pay the check and meet me out there so that we could go somewhere else to talk. I waited for almost 30 minutes, D, and when I pulled out and looked inside the diner, she was on the phone."

"What?" he asked.

"Yeah, I don't know what that was all about, but I figured it was more important than what we were discussing." She sighed disappointedly.

"Which was?"

Reaching into the medicine cabinet to get the peroxide, ointment, and bandages, she settled down on the toilet top. "Mama had this positive pregnancy test result paper that she practically flung in my face while believing everything that was on it. She barely let me get a word in until I've had enough and then that's when everything fell apart. DeTroyt," she said, working on her wound. "I've never in my 25 years yelled at my mother, but I was furious! After Kaleb started pre-k, I promised her that I would go back to school and oh my goodness, that paper just put her in an uproar!" Finally finished patching herself up, she stated, "I don't know where or who it came from!" She paused for a minute. "DeTroyt, do you have any enemies?" With that, she thought, *Stephon!*

"Um, no," he replied. "I can't say that I do."

"Okay."

Curious, he asked why.

"Because all of this has to stem from something… somewhere… someone!"

"Well," DeTroyt said. "You know I was also calling about church. We're having a youth revival starting Sunday night, and I thought maybe you wanted to go with me."

"Well, I don't—"

"Shae, they are gonna have some of everybody there. Plus, I believe God is really gonna bless that place."

There was an awkward pause and then DeTroyt continued. "I know that I told you when you were ready to let me know, but I really believe that you are meant to be at this meeting next week."

After sitting there for a moment to think about it, she let out a deep sigh before replying. "Okay, D. I'll go with you. But I can't promise you the entire week."

"Hey, one day is better than no day at all," DeTroyt replied.

"Yeah, look I really need to go. Do you mind if I call you later? I have something that I need to take care of."

"Sure. You can call me later. I was getting ready for my dinner date with Erica and I thought about the revival and called to ask you."

LaShae said goodbye to DeTroyt and ended the call. She then grabbed her keys and went out to start her car. She backed out from her driveway and onto the street. She was still amazed and shocked by what happened earlier. Not really wanting to stay home, she called Keven to see if he felt like company.

Chapter Thirteen

Keven

THE STORM

LaShae dialed Keven's number as she sat at the red light.

"Hello?" came the voice on the other end.

At first she wasn't going to say anything, but she thought better of it. "Hello, is Keven there?" LaShae asked, still a little confused. *Who was this person?*

Very snotty, she replied, "Honey, Keven is unavailable right now." *Click.*

LaShae was thrown aback when she heard a dial tone in her ear. "What? She did not just hang up on me!" she yelled from within the privacy of her car as she continued to drive in the direction of Keven's home. Needless to say, she was a tad bit frustrated now, especially after another girl just answered his phone... again. Not to mention how familiar her voice sounded... *but that couldn't be her.*

She pushed that thought out of her head when she pulled into the yard and did not see any other cars there but his. She sat in her car for a few minutes with the lights off, debating whether to get out or go home. The decision was made for her when she saw a figure emerge from Keven's house. She couldn't make out exactly who it was, but it definitely wasn't a female and they were coming in her direction.

LaShae put her car into reverse and was about to press the gas when she finally saw the face. It was *him*. Their eyes remained locked as he approached the front of her car and passed on into the night. LaShae made sure that he was completely gone before she jumped out and ran inside.

Once in the doorway, she gasped at what she saw. Keven was lying in a puddle of blood that looked as if it came from his side. He clutched the telephone in one hand and was holding his side with the other. His lips were moving and his eyes beckoned her to move closer, so she did. She leaned down close to him so that she could hear what he was saying.

"My... chele... " His voice was barely a whisper before it faded out.

"Mychele? Please don't try to say anything," she said, trying to stay calm. She checked his breathing. She could see the rise and fall of his chest. Thank God he was still breathing. LaShae heard the voice of what sounded like the operator on the line. She quickly took the phone out of Keven's hand and began to tell her what happened.

"Hello. Hello?" she said into the receiver.

"911, please state your emergency," came the operator.

Hysterically, she yelled, "I need help! My fiancé has been stabbed. I–I walked in and found him lying on the floor in a pool of blood! Please hurry! Please!"

"Ma'am, is he still alive?"

"Yes, he's breathing… very staggered though. Please hurry! Please!" LaShae begged. She was in tears now.

"Okay, ma'am. What's the address?"

"Um, sure, sure." LaShae provided the address and asked if they could please hurry.

"We have a unit on its way right now. Do you feel like you are in danger, ma'am? Is the intruder still there?"

"No, umm… no, I don't think so."

"I'm going to stay connected until the unit arrives, okay, ma'am?"

"Thank you! Thank you so much." LaShae placed the phone on speaker and sat down next to Keven as she began to talk to him. She tried to reassure him that everything was going to be okay in spite of.

Keven was moaning in pain. There were tears flowing from his eyes, and he looked at her with total fear in his eyes.

"Hold on, baby. The paramedics are on the way." She could hear the ambulance in the distance.

"They're almost here, sweetie. Please, just hold on."

Keven tried to speak, but she wouldn't allow it. For the first time after arriving at the house, LaShae looked around. The house was a total wreck, as though there was a huge struggle.

"Oh my goodness," was all she managed to get out when heard the paramedics rushing through the door with their tools. LaShae stepped back to give them room. Carefully, they cleaned and wrapped Keven's wound and placed an oxygen mask over his mouth and nose before lifting him onto the gurney. They fastened him onto the gurney and hurried out the door. LaShae was close behind.

"Ma'am," said one of the paramedics who happened to be a

black female about 5'5". "Ma'am, I'm sorry, but you won't be able to ride with him. We have a lot more work to do, okay?"

LaShae started to protest but decided against it. "Okay. I'll, uh, I'll drive." She ran to her car and jumped behind the wheel. By the time she started her car, the ambulance had started down the driveway. She quickly put her car in gear and caught up with them.

Her phone rang, but this time it was her mom.

"Mama! Look, I can't talk right now. I'm on my way to the hospital with Keven. He was stabbed or something and left for dead."

She heard a loud gasp come through the phone. "What? I'm on my way!"

Click.

"But—"

She hung up before LaShae could say which hospital they were going to. Of course, there was only one major hospital in town…

LaShae prayed like never before. But then her mind traveled back to the name that Keven said… *MyChele. What does she have to do with this? I saw Stephon come out of the house and pass my car. What on earth did Keven mean?* She pondered that question until she reached the hospital.

Upon arrival, she saw the paramedics rush Keven through the emergency doors. She parked in the closet space and ran inside. They had already taken Keven to the back so that he could be prepped for surgery.

LaShae rushed to the triage nurse and the nurse kind of gave her an unknowing look. LaShae repeated the question a little slower this time. "Ke-ven Mit-chell. Where is he?"

The nurse, now thinking that she just called her stupid, asked, "Who might you be?"

"I'm his fiancée. Is there any papers that I need to fill out or something?"

The nurse, whose name tag read Yota, had a grin on her face that seemed way too revealing, as if she knew something. She looked a little young to be standing behind a nurses station, but nowadays they all were.

"His fiancée, you say? I'm sorry but she was just here and filled out everything. That's why he went back so quickly." The nurse then shook her head and turned to walk away.

"Wait a minute," LaShae called after her. "What did you say?"

Now seeming to have an attitude, Nurse Yota replied, "I *said* his fiancée is with him already." With that, she turned to leave.

Turning to face the door that they may have rolled Keven through, LaShae marched through them also.

"I'll find him myself. What fiancée is she talking about? There better be only one and that one better be me. I didn't pray this pain away for noth… ing." LaShae's voice trailed off as she approached the door.

What she saw made her stop dead in her tracks. MyChele was hovering over Keven as if he was her man or something. *But how did she know that he was here?* LaShae knew that MyChele cared about him and all, but goodness. This was overdoing it a little… She was crying crocodile tears and holding his hand and rubbing his head. LaShae was so speechless and lost in thought that she hadn't noticed that the ER doctor had been trying to get her attention. He finally succeeded.

"Ma'am, do you need some help? Are you looking for anyone?"

Mychele looked up to see LaShae standing in the hallway staring at her. For a few seconds, they stared at each other. The doctor broke the spell by clearing his throat.

Not wanting to cause a scene, LaShae turned back to the doctor. "No. No, thank you. Um, I probably came to the wrong hospital." With that, she turned and ran out of the double doors that led back to ER admission. She could hear MyChele calling to her, but she kept running.

When she reached her car, she got in and sat for a minute. Her blood was boiling so much she could spit fire. LaShae, starting to drive off, stopped when Jasmyn pulled up. She jumped out of her car and rushed over to her daughter's side. "Hey, what's wrong? Is Keven alright?"

LaShae put her car into park, got out, and hugged her mom tightly. "Oh, Mama," she began. "They have Keven in surgery, but when I got to the room, Mychele was all over him like he was her man or something. I didn't want to cause a scene, so I ran out and was about to leave when you pulled up."

Jasmyn stepped back and looked at LaShae in disbelief. "So you just left her hovering over your man? Baby, that is not like you. By now, you would've had a handful of her hair as you dragged her down this sidewalk. What's going on with you?"

LaShae smiled a little, knowing her mother was telling the truth. But for some reason, she didn't have that fight for Keven in her anymore. "Mama, I don't know. But since you're here, can you please stay with him? I need some air. This has been one crazy day."

Jasmyn looked at her daughter for a minute before responding. "Yes, honey, I will stay. And for the record, I believe you when you said you weren't pregnant. We talk about everything. I don't know why I would think that subject would be any different."

"Thanks, Mama," she replied before getting back into her car. "Thanks for everything. I love you."

"I love you too," Jasmyn stated. She gave her daughter another comforting hug before walking toward the hospital ER doors.

LaShae got back into her car and started the engine.

As LaShae drove off, she could see MyChele standing under the ambulatory entrance with her hands over her face. In her rearview mirror, she saw Jasmyn walk up to Mychele and then they both went inside. LaShae was able to make it out of the parking lot of the hospital, but she couldn't go any further due to the massive amount of tears that was blocking her view. She pulled over to a well-lit service station to try and calm her overworked nerves. She was already hysterical and freaking out over finding Keven half-dead, not to mention seeing his attacker, but now this?

Should I call the police? What if they think that I did it because I was there? Then what? I would lose my son. Our son. But I didn't do anything so why should I be afraid? LaShae's mind was running wild with so many thoughts till it was impossible for her to think straight.

- LaShae waited until she was able to speak clearly before calling DeTroyt.

"Hello," he answered

"Hello, DeTroyt. I, um… I really need to see you tonight. I don't know if I could make it through the night without at least talking to someone. May I come over?" Not that she wasn't worried about what was going on with Keven, but what she saw and having that nurse tell her that his fiancée was back there with him already was too much for her. This was not even mentioning her encounter with Stephon Knight.

There was a slight pause before he answered. "Sure you can. Just give me about an hour. Okay?"

"Sure. Um, that's fine," LaShae replied, a little disappointed. "Listen, I'm going to stop and get a taco or something. Would you like something as well? All of this excitement has made me very hungry."

DeTroyt paused again. "No, thank you. I've already eaten." There was yet another pause. "So, I'll see you in about an hour, okay? And you can fill me in on your excitement when you get here."

"Okay. Thank you, DeTroyt. See you in an hour." She hung up the phone and started on her journey to the closest taco stand.

She then pulled into the parking lot and walked up to the window to place her order.

"Honey, who was that on the phone?" Erica asked as she walked over to DeTroyt.

"Oh, uh, that was LaShae. You remember LaShae, don't you, honey?" he asked nervously.

"Yes, of course I do. How can I forget? You talk about her all the time. She's the one that you saved in that car accident three or four months ago, right?"

"Yeah, that's her," he answered, not realizing that he talked about her that much to the point where it was all someone would remember about him. DeTroyt walked back over to the couch where they were once sitting and watching a movie prior to LaShae calling.

Erica, turning in his direction, watched DeTroyt get comfortable on the couch from her spot in the kitchen. He turned to her and motioned for her to come sit next to him.

Hesitant, she did, but not before asking what the call was about.

DeTroyt replied to her question carefully but honestly. "Erica, ever since the accident, Shae has been trying to think of ways to repay me for saving her life. I told her that God placed me at that intersection for her and she should be thanking Him, not me. I also invited her to church and gave her numbers to the church and here if she needed a ride." DeTroyt took Erica's hand in his. "LaShae and I are like brothers and sisters. She can pretty much talk to me about anything. I don't push her away when she needs to talk because that's my opportunity to talk about Christ to her as well." He let out a deep sigh before continuing.

"Tonight, she called to see if she could come over to talk. It sounds as if she'd been crying. I told her to give me about an hour, so she went to get something to eat and will be on her way after that."

Erica sat with her eyes frozen on DeTroyt. "So you're seriously going to allow another woman to come into this house? Alone?" she asked in disbelief.

"Erica, honey, please…"

Snatching her hands away, she got up from the couch and started gathering her things. "Don't you 'Erica, honey' me, DeTroyt Maning. Does the pastor know that you company people of her *kind*?"

Jumping up from the couch, DeTroyt walked over to where Erica stood with her belongings in her hands. "What do you mean 'people of her kind'?"

"I've had her checked out. The things that I found out are very disturbing. She does not need to be alone in the presence of a man," she said as she snorted her nose in the air.

"What? And you can? Everyone is entitled to change. It doesn't matter what she used to be and what she used to do, that's the past and we're living in the present, striving to be with God in the future. What's your beef? I thought you were bigger than that." DeTroyt had finally begun to see what Erica was all about. If the women in his life, new or old, were not from a rich and powerful family, she would look down on them and wanted absolutely nothing to do with them.

"Erica, we've been together for three years and engaged for one; if you really love me like you say you do, then my friends would be your friends. I've accepted your friends for who they are. I didn't go snooping around to see what they used to be or had done in their past. That's the past and—"

"Well, DeTroyt, I'm sorry but I just can't accept someone like her being our friend."

"What? But Er—"

"And if you can't respect my opinion in this relationship, then we don't need to be together. I will not have a whore as my friend and neither will I have you as a husband for associating yourself with such trash."

All DeTroyt could do was lower his head in dismay. He looked up when he heard Erica open the door. They stared at each other.

"So the cross of redemption means absolutely nothing to you then and neither does this relationship?"

Erica lowered her head only to look back up with tears in her eyes. "Goodbye, DeTroyt," she said softly as she walked out of his life forever.

DeTroyt stood there staring at the spot where his beloved fiancée stood just moments before. After realizing she wasn't coming back, he started putting things away. The fruit tray, the glasses that they'd used, and the bottle of sparkling cider.

DeTroyt had prepared a steak dinner with potatoes and mixed vegetables. Dinner had gone well. Their conversation consisted of their future together and how many children they wanted to have. After dinner, they decided to watch the movie that Erica had brought over. Right in the middle of it was when things fell apart...

"Maybe she'll get over it and apologize. Then again, if she feels that strongly about befriending an ex- whatever and trying to lead them to Christ, then she is the wrong one for me," DeTroyt said, thinking out loud. "Maybe it's for the best," he concluded as he continued to clear the dishes and load the dishwasher.

Chapter Fourteen

La Shae

FRIEND OR FOE?

LaShae had gotten her taco salad with salsa and sour cream and also a hard shell taco with a soda. By the time she finished her taco salad, she was stuffed. She put the taco away in a carryout bag and started on her way to DeTroyt's house which was less than five minutes away.

Her phone rang as soon as she got back in the car. She answered it without looking at the caller ID.

"Hello?"

"Shae, it's me. Please don't hang up. Let me explain what you saw at the hospital."

"MyChele, you don't have to waste your breath because whatever you have to say will not change the fact that you were there in my place," LaShae said, getting angrier at the thought.

"Shae, it's not what you thought. You know Keven and I are as close. We're as close as me and you used to be and…"

"And what, Chele? You took it upon yourself to pretend like you were his fiancée? Did you do all of his admission papers to make me look like an idiot?"

"What? LaShae Wilson, what are you talking about? I don't know anything about no paperwork! The lady at the desk said to go on back with him because everything was done already. I figured you did it by phone and you were coming!"

She paused for what seemed to be forever. A soft sniffle filled the silence.

"Chele, what's wrong?" LaShae asked, fearing the worst. When MyChele said nothing, LaShae repeated her question.

"LaShae, I don't know how to tell you this."

"Just tell me!" she was yelling hysterically now.

LaShae had made it to DeTroyt's house and was almost at the door when MyChele gave her the news.

"Shae, Keven didn't make it. He lost too much blood and the knife wound was so deep, it punctured an artery. When they cleaned him up, he had knife marks all over him. It's as if whoever did this meant to kill him by butchering him to death."

"No!" she screamed at the top of her lungs.

DeTroyt heard a horrific scream and opened the door just in

time to catch LaShae. He saw the cell phone in her hand and took it. He introduced himself to the caller and asked what happened. Mychele filled DeTroyt in on the news about Keven. DeTroyt gave his condolences and ended their conversation. He placed LaShae on the couch to rest while he sat on the love seat and yet again, watched and prayed over her.

When LaShae came to, she realized that she was lying on DeTroyt's couch with an ice pack on her head. She gave him a little smile. Just to see him sitting across from her on the love seat watching her and making sure she was okay brought back memories.

"This scene looks familiar." Her head was throbbing. "Mmm, what happened?" she asked, rubbing the back of her head.

"How about you just take it easy for right now… How does that sound?" replied DeTroyt.

She found out as the night went on that DeTroyt had spoken with MyChele and Jasmyn after she had passed out after hearing about Keven's death, which saved LaShae the pain of having to do so for the most part.

Little did he know, this was only the beginning of the story. LaShae had been a victim of threats and a witness to a murder.

LaShae thought for a moment if she should tell DeTroyt about her day. After all, that was why she wanted to come over in the first place. Stephon had threatened to hurt her and Kaleb if she were to say anything to anyone about her conversation, but she knew that she could trust DeTroyt not to say anything.

"DeTroyt, I know who killed Keven." LaShae looked as though to say *please don't freak out.*

Well, he did just that. He leaped up from the love seat and plopped onto the couch by LaShae. Panic was written all over his face.

"What? Are you sure?" he asked. "We've got to tell the police!" He grabbed the cordless phone out of its cradle. He got so much as the number nine punched in when LaShae grabbed the phone from him.

"No! We can't go to the police. Not yet."

DeTroyt looked a bit confused. "Why? Shae, if you know who did this, you should notify the authorities."

Sighing in disgust and regretting that she even brought the matter up, she said, "Listen, if I go to anyone, he will come after me and Kaleb."

"Who?" DeTroyt asked, his voice a little louder than his normal speaking tone. Reluctantly, she told him everything from beginning to end. By the time she finished her story, DeTroyt was pacing the floor so vigorously she thought he would burn a hole through the carpet. He stopped to look at her before commenting on what she just told him. "So this guy, this Stephon person, do you think he's the one who sent me all of those messages?" Over the past couple of months, ever so often, DeTroyt will get notes left on his car or voicemail messages on his phone to leave LaShae alone "or else." Each time, he would take them to Detective Jones for him to investigate.

LaShae shrugged and indicated that she didn't know. "It's possible though. But why would he still mess with you if he's found me already? This is insane."

LaShae got off the couch and stood over by the window. It was midnight, but in DeTroyt's neighborhood, it seemed like it was 12 in the afternoon. Cars were pulling in and out and people were standing or sitting on their porch just enjoying each other's company. The neighborhood seemed very decent with no crime whatsoever.

She turned back to DeTroyt who was sitting on the love seat again. He looked a little disturbed. Guessing with everything that had gone on with LaShae since they met, she was surprised he hadn't just left her standing to deal with it all on her own. But he didn't leave her and that was what made her care so much about him. She pushed those thoughts out of her head because she knew, without a doubt, nothing will ever happen. She went over to the love seat and sat next to DeTroyt.

"Crazy, huh?" she asked.

"What's crazy?" he questioned.

"Everything!"

"Oh, yeah," he said, letting out a slight chuckle.

"It doesn't seem like we're talking about the same thing," LaShae stated. "What's wrong?" she asked, truly concerned.

DeTroyt sat quietly for a moment. He began rubbing his palms together as though he was nervous about something. Finally, he replied, "It's nothing that I can't handle… really."

LaShae wasn't buying it. "DeTroyt, we are better than that. Our friendship is a two-way street. I'm here for you, and you are here for me."

He let out a deep sigh. "Erica and I had a slight disagreement on something that was very important to me. Because I didn't take her side on it and stood my ground, she just walked out."

"Oh, I'm so sorry," LaShae responded, placing her hand on his back.

"Well, who and what God has for me will be for me," he stated with confidence. Changing the subject, he added, "It has been a long day for both of us, mostly you. Let's call it a night. You need your rest." DeTroyt got up from the couch, stretched, and yawned.

LaShae followed suit. "Yeah, I guess you're right. I have a big day tomorrow, and I'm gonna need every ounce of energy to get through it."

"You can sleep in my bed, and I'll sleep out here on the couch." He showed her where the bathroom and bedroom were located. "Make yourself at home. There's a fridge full of stuff in case you are a midnight snacker like me," he said with a smile on his face.

"Ok, thank you," she replied. She gave him a hug and scurried off to the bathroom. By the time she got out of the bathroom, DeTroyt had already retired to the couch. She stood in the hallway entrance and looked at how peaceful he looked as he slept before turning to retire to the bedroom for the night.

That night was the first night in a long time that LaShae was able to rest from the cares of her life without any interruption. She slept like a baby; DeTroyt, on the other hand, tossed and turned all night long. All he could think about was Erica. For him, morning couldn't come quick enough.

After cooking breakfast and making sure that she was able to drive, DeTroyt finally let LaShae go home. Despite her head and back pains, LaShae convinced him that she was okay.

Once she got home, she tried to call Mychele, but each time there was no answer. LaShae had left several voicemails, each with no return phone call, not even a text. LaShae continued to call her throughout the night, but still nothing.

DeTroyt came over to visit on Saturday, which also was the day before the youth revival began for that week. By this time, all of Keven's funeral arrangements had been made. LaShae and Jasmyn had to go on Monday to do the final paperwork and pick out a plot. Jasmyn, LaShae, and MyChele were pretty much the only family Keven had left. His father left him and his mother when he was six years old. By the time Keven was sixteen, his mother had been diagnosed with cervical cancer which took her life by the time he was eighteen. Since then, he had been doing it on his own.

Keven had tried searching for his father after that, only to find that he'd been killed in a tragic logging accident. The morgue was unable to locate the next of kin, so they cremated the body. From that point on, Jasmyn had been a mother figure and Mychele and LaShae were his "play" sisters though Keven and LaShae's status had changed when she got pregnant with Kaleb. They knew they cared about each other a lot but having Kaleb was the icing on the cake. Well, for LaShae, at least…

Keven denied Kaleb from day one. LaShae understood that he was not ready to be a parent, but neither was she. That cut extremely deep. Now Kaleb will never truly know his father. Keven was a good man, but because he didn't have a father figure, he was a little lost in that category. For the past few months though, Keven had been trying to be the best father to Kaleb, which made his memories of his father even better.

Jasmyn and DeTroyt helped LaShae pack up Keven's furniture and clothes to give to those in need. He had two vehicles, an SUV and a convertible, that he never drove. They donated those to the home for battered women who were very grateful. Believe it or not, so was LaShae. She couldn't bear to watch his belongings not be put to good use. Yes, she could have kept both vehicles and people would probably judge her because she donated them, but who cares? She sure as hell didn't.

Chapter Fifteen

Carla and DeTroyt

THE CALL

"Hello?" DeTroyt answered, sounding a bit frustrated. He hadn't slept really well the night before and was with LaShae all day helping her and Jasmyn with Keven's things. Though they tried to talk her into waiting before donating everything, she decided against it. So he was a bit edgy.

"Hi, um DeTroyt? This is Carla. Did I catch you at a bad time?" she asked cautiously.

Her call caught him off guard. Whatever mood he was in, quickly changed. "Carla!" he said, trying to sound more upbeat. "Listen, I want to apologize for my rudeness the other evening. I was just so…" he paused, trying to find the right word to say.

"Overwhelmed," she filled in.

"Well, yes," he replied.

"DeTroyt, I completely understand and I would like to apologize to you as well for actually thinking that by me popping up to see you, that all of the ill feelings between us would just… dissipate. I didn't mean to overstep my boundaries by speaking to Vicki without your approval. I just really wanted to see her. She's beautiful, D, simply beautiful. You've done an outstanding job with raising her."

"Yes, she is a wonderful young girl, but I'm not sure if I like where that last statement you made is heading," he said, throwing the bait and hoping she'd bite.

And she did.

"Well, you have done an outstanding job," she said. What she really wanted to say was, *No, give her to me! I'm her mother!* Instead she simply stated, "I just thought that me and you can share the responsibility now."

DeTroyt, infuriated, plainly said, "No. You told me to take care of her because you could not. I will not allow you to come, 11 years later, when you feel like you're ready to be a mama. I sacrificed ALL of myself and my dreams when you left her on my grandmother's porch. I will send you pictures, but I refuse to share ANY responsibility with you. I'm responsible, always have been, always will be."`

"D, please! I know you're angry with me and I don't blame you. I walked away from both of you, but I had no choice!"

There was an awkward pause and Carla broke the silence. "Can we meet for coffee or breakfast in the morning? You pick the place, and I'll pay the tab." She hoped this would at least give him more time to think about her proposal a little while longer. "What do you say?" she pushed.

"I'll call you in the morning. Good night, Carla." He hung up without another word.

Carla was pleased and was grinning from ear to ear. "You are just where I want you."

The morning didn't come quick enough for Carla, but it came too quickly for DeTroyt. After dropping off Vicki at school, DeTroyt called Carla and told her to meet him at the mom and pop coffee shop on Main Street around 8:30 a.m. and she agreed. He was not looking forward to having this conversation, and she was not going to convince him to change his mind.

When he arrived, Carla was already seated and motioned him over to the table.

"Wow, you're early," he said, stating her punctuality.

"And you're right on time," she said of his tardiness. They both smiled.

"I was waiting until you arrived to place the order. What would you like?" she asked.

DeTroyt, curious as to where this was all leading to, declined the food and ordered a cup of decaf coffee instead.

"Decaf?" exclaimed Carla. "What is that gonna do for you other than keep you warm?" she asked sarcastically.

"Carla, we are not here to discuss decaf coffee and its side effects, we are here to discuss Vicki," he said impatiently.

"You're right," she replied. "It's simple, D. I want Vicki back in my life. It's been pure hell knowing that I have a daughter in this world who doesn't even know that I exist."

"Yeah, and it's my problem because?" This time, it was his turn to be rude.

Carla pursed her lips before speaking. "You act like I wanted to walk away from her. DeTroyt, *I had no other choice!*" She wanted to scream that at the top of her lungs until he got it, but she didn't want to cause a scene and it probably wouldn't do any good no way. He was so bullheaded.

"You keep saying that, but you had me, Carla! *You had me!* We could have done this together!" he exclaimed, pounding his fist on the table.

The noise startled Carla and she responded accordingly. "No, we couldn't have. My father was ready to throw you so far under the jail because of this," she replied to him.

DeTroyt looked at her, unable to hide his expressions which now turned to rage. Carla's father, the "Honorable Judge Stoneybrook," hated the ground that DeTroyt walked on. He always told Carla that DeTroyt was from "the other side" of the tracks and that she was too good for him. And when Carla became pregnant with Vicki, it was all the judge could do to not arrest him for what he called "nonconsensual sex" since DeTroyt was a few years older than Carla. At the time of her pregnancy, she was 16 and he was 19. He failed 8th grade, and his birthday was later in the year so he had to start school a year after.

"Daddy said if I didn't get rid of this bastard child, the law would have you thrown in jail and the key to your cell in the ocean with the sharks. By the time he found out, I was already three and a half months too late for an abortion. That's why I left without a trace until I had her and I had to bring her back to you."

DeTroyt, still looking at her as though *she* were her father, the "Honorable Judge Storybrook." The waitress brought his coffee and Carla's breakfast, breaking the monotony at the table.

They both thanked the waitress and once she was gone, Carla finished her story.

DeTroyt held up a hand before she could begin. "So you're telling me your awesome dad wanted you to get rid of his only grandchild because of me?" He couldn't believe what he was hearing. "But you couldn't because you were too far along so they sent you away to have the baby just to bring her back to me so that you can go to school while I take care of the baby as if I had no plans of my own to accomplish?" he continued bitterly. "Now that you're stable and well-established with your lawyer husband, you want me to give my daughter that I've raised since she was an infant, fresh out of your womb, back to you?"

Carla was embarrassed by how everything sounded now, so she remained silent.

"Well, Carla, I must be on my way. Enjoy your breakfast," he said, pushing his chair back. "This is for my coffee." He reached into his pocket and withdrew $5. "Have a great life. Now I don't owe you anything." With that, DeTroyt turned and walked out of the diner.

Carla, fishing her phone out of her purse, placed another call. "Time for plan B," she said before disconnecting the call. She finished her breakfast in silence while waiting for her next move.

Chapter Sixteen

La Shae

THE CONFRONTATION

That Sunday night, as LaShae listened to what the minister said, she felt a calmness within. It was something she'd never felt before.

After church, Kaleb, Vicki, and LaShae met for the first time. She had heard as much about Vicki as DeTroyt had heard about Kaleb.

"Are you my daddy's new girlfriend?" Vicki asked LaShae.

LaShae was taken aback by her question.

"Erica, uh excuse me, Mz. Erica didn't like me very much. She would tell me that the clothes my daddy bought me were ugly, and I blended right in. When we went to visit her at her house, she'd make me stay in the car." She paused for a minute and looked at LaShae as if to study her before asking, "Are you mean too?"

Just for the fun of it, LaShae gave her a look of disapproval that nearly scared the poor child to tears. All Kaleb could do was laugh for he knew that was not his mother's character.

"No, sweetie, I'm not mean. In fact, I know Ms. Erica was wrong about you blending in with your clothes. You are very pretty and so are your clothes, but you have to believe that for yourself too." LaShae knelt down in front of her so that their eyes could meet. "As the saying goes, 'true beauty is beneath the skin.' This means no matter what you look like on the outside, if your personality is beautiful, then so are you. Okay?"

"Okay. Thanks Mz. LaShae," she replied with a big smile on her face.

LaShae gave her a hug, but before letting go, she said, "You don't have to call me 'Mz.' LaShae, Ms. LaShae would do just fine. And to answer your question, no, I'm not your daddy's new girlfriend. He and I are just friends, okay?"

Vicki stared at LaShae for a moment before replying. "Okay, Mz. I mean, Ms. LaShae."

Vicki and Kaleb went to the dining area to get a plate of some sort to eat. LaShae patiently waited for DeTroyt to emerge from what seemed like a deep conversation with one of the mothers there.

"Yes, ma'am. I sure will," she heard him say as DeTroyt watched the little old lady walk out of the door.

DeTroyt was laughing by the time he approached LaShae.

"What's so funny?" she asked, laughing as well.

"Mother Benson is already making us a couple. She said, 'That young lady right there, DeTroyt, is going to make you a good wife one day'." He laughed, mimicking her. "She continued with, 'Yep, she gon' be somebody. Watch my word, ya hea?' Then she turned to me and said, 'Now you go on back over there before she thinks I'm trying to pick you up. Go on now'." That conversation literally made DeTroyt's night.

"So hea' I is," he concluded.

"Wow," was all LaShae could say.

DeTroyt grabbed her hand and led her to one of the pews toward the front. As they approached the pew, he turned and asked, "Did you enjoy the service?"

She nodded yes. "It's more than what I expected. I could probably get used to this." She sat down where he insisted.

DeTroyt sat down beside her. "Listen, LaShae. I know it's hard for you right now with everything that you're going through and all, but listen to me… If you need anything, I mean absolutely anything… someone to watch Kaleb, or take you somewhere, money, whatever it is… I'm here for you, okay? In spite of how we met, you're my friend and I care about what happens to you."

LaShae couldn't hold back the tears of gratitude. She knew she could always count on DeTroyt to be there for her. These last few weeks he has proven to be a true friend. She fell into his arms as the tears consumed her.

"Why? Why did he have to leave me? Things had started getting better between us," she sobbed. "We were engaged and he finally took responsibility for his child… our child. Kaleb loves him so much. They went fishing and to the park together." She said between sobs. "They shopped and watched movies. I mean they hung out more than he and I did." She had to giggle at that statement because Keven was always coming by to pick Kaleb up for something… saying, "it was boys' day out, no girls allowed."

DeTroyt tightly embraced her, letting her know that it was okay. "Shae, I'm so sorry. I am very sorry. Just know that I'm here for you."

"Thank you. I'm just grateful Kaleb and Keven got the chance to know each other before this… this happened." The pain was too much for her to bear. Even though she had come to church tonight, her spirit still felt heavy.

At that moment, she remembered the guest speaker saying to "cast all your cares on Him, for He cares for you." But how can she do that? He also said that "God will not put anymore on you than you can bear…" Well… realizing they were still in the sanctuary, LaShae remembered that it was getting late so she started gathering her things to go.

He agreed.

LaShae really wasn't up to meeting anyone else right now, so she asked DeTroyt if he could go and get the kids. Little did she and DeTroyt know… they were being watched.

Once DeTroyt was out of earshot, LaShae heard footsteps coming up behind her. "So, who are you?" a female voice asked.

LaShae spun around to see a tall, slim lady looking down on her as if she wanted to slit her throat.

"Who wants to know?" LaShae asked, standing to meet the woman's gaze.

"I do," she said, this time with an attitude.

Trying to keep her composure, especially in the church, LaShae politely asked, "And just why do you *need* to know?"

"I don't, and it really doesn't matter." The tall figure opened her mouth to say something else when DeTroyt approached.

"Erica, what are you doing here? I didn't expect to see you anymore, especially after our conversation the other night," he said as he emerged from the dining hall with the kids. There was a certain look about him in her presence. A disturbed look.

Startled, Erica turned in DeTroyt's direction. "DeTroyt," she said in more of a statement than a greeting.

"DeTroyt, honey. Erica and I were just getting acquainted with each other, weren't we darling?" she asked in a fake French accent. Turning toward Erica, she stated, still in her fake French accent, "You know you startled me when you came up behind me and demanded to know my name and what my business was here." Her gaze never left Erica's.

"Well, I saw you two all hugged up together and I got curious. I really did—"

"You know, Erica, is it?" LaShae spoke in her normal voice. "Those games are for children; therefore, I will not stoop to your level of intelligence. If you *must* know, my fiancé was killed four days ago and being the friend that DeTroyt is, he was comforting me." LaShae drew in a long breath before exhaling. "So let me make this suggestion to you; if you want to know something, come to me like a woman and we can talk about it like women because you don't know me at all to be walking up on me and demanding information from me."

"Ladies," DeTroyt tried to intercept, but he was just ignored.

"Oh, but I do, Ms. Wilson," said Erica. "I know all I need to know about you, and I have a problem with what I found out about you. I would like it if you stopped hanging around my man."

"And I suggest that you get your head out of the clouds as though you are untouchable because, baby, you can be brought back down to Earth." With that, LaShae took Kaleb's hand and began walking out of the church with tears streaming down her face.

"Ms. LaShae!" she heard Vicki call after her. Vicki turned to Erica and stated, "That's why she's prettier than you, Mzzzzz Erica!" With that, Vicki turned and began running in LaShae's direction.

The expression on Erica's face was priceless and LaShae tried to hold in her laugh.

"Victoria Shonta Maning, you get back here and apologize right now, young lady," DeTroyt demanded.

However, Vicki had already made it to LaShae and was hugging her. LaShae hugged her in return.

"Please don't leave Ms. Shae. I really like having you around. You are so much nicer than *she* is." She accented with her nose turned up in the air and her eyes in rotation.

"Now, Vicki, you know that was not nice. It doesn't matter how angry you get at a person, you should never be ugly to them, okay? I appreciate you showing me how you feel toward me, but there is a nicer way to do it." LaShae tried to be as gentle as possible with a straight face.

Vicki began to pout. "I know and I'm sorry, but she was mean to you."

"Listen, you need to go and apologize to Mz. Erica before you get into any more trouble." LaShae hugged her again.

DeTroyt called her name again and Vicki turned and started walking back toward her father and Erica. She heard Vicki apologize and Erica's smart comment toward her. To keep from involving herself in the issue anymore than she was already, she and Kaleb walked out of the sanctuary doors and toward her car.

"Now that's enough, Erica!" stated DeTroyt. "It's bad enough that you come in here spying on me and insulting my friend who—"

"Who's an ex-hooker," Erica stated with confidence and one hand on her hip.

"Daddy, what's a hooker?" Vicki asked.

"Sweetheart, go over there until I'm finished talking, okay?" He pointed Vicki toward the pews on the other side of the church sanctuary.

Turning back to Erica, DeTroyt was furious. "How dare you make such accusations about LaShae that way and in front of my daughter!"

"Well, the child has to learn one way or another," she replied nonchalantly.

DeTroyt felt his old self coming out and had to say a quick prayer of repentance for his thoughts. "I will not stand here and let you insult my daughter's intelligence nor my friend's past lifestyle. For that matter, I don't want you near Vicki or myself again." He started to walk away, but then turned to face Erica. "You know, I thought we would be able to work things out but I see you can't get over your way of thinking that you're better than everyone else. When is it going to end? You act as though you are a sinless person who has no flaws, hidden or knowingly. You have got to get over yourself and your jealousy issues. If I'm going to be a man of God, then I have to treat everyone the way that God intends for us to treat them and I need a real woman of God by my side that truly understands this. I cannot be married to someone who, when I leave the room, confronts innocent people. And for what, Erica? That's not godly, that's jealousy and a hindrance to what God told me to do and I can't have any part of that. I just can't. So it's over."

With that statement, he took Vicki and walked away from Erica.

There was nothing that Erica could say in return, so she too walked out of the sanctuary. She figured she would give him a little time to cool off and things will be back to normal between them. At least that's what she'd hoped. *Erica, what were you thinking?!* she scolded herself.

LaShae was getting Kaleb settled in his seatbelt when she heard her name being yelled across the church ground.

"Hey, LaShae!"

She turned to see DeTroyt and Vicki running toward her.

"Hey, what's up?" She noticed that he was struggling for air. *Lack of exercise?* was what she wanted to ask, but instead she asked, "Where's Erica?"

"Gone. Listen, I am so sorry for what happened there. I had no idea that she would even be here." He was so apologetic and sincere, but truth be told, she really wasn't in the mood for apologies. "Would you like for us to follow you home? Given the circumstances of the last few months and all."

Flattered, but also aware of how late it was, she declined, but not before she said her peace. "Listen, D, I don't know what's going on between you and Erica, but I really wish that you both would leave me out of it. I accept your apology because I know it's not your fault as to how disrespectful she acted, but just to forewarn you, she doesn't ever need to come at me again in that manner. Tonight, I respected God's house, but if we were on the streets, I couldn't promise you that I would've walked away. How dare she say those things about me, especially in front of my son?" LaShae felt her blood begin to rise again so she cut the conversation short. "As for following us home, thank you, but we'll be fine. I will let you know when we make it." She gave them both a hug before joining Kaleb in the car. She gave them both a warm smile, started the engine, and pulled off. Before heading toward his truck, DeTroyt and Vicki watched as LaShae drove off the church grounds. Kaleb waved from the back window.

Everything about this night was clear except the thoughts flowing in Erica's head. Thoughts about the conversation that she and DeTroyt had the other week as well as how quickly he came to LaShae's defense tonight tossed and turned in her head like a nightmare.

"The nerve of him to choose her over me," Erica stated to no one. She was in her car by the time DeTroyt and Vicki had made it to Lashae's car. Erica saw the whole thing. "Who does he think he is? I don't care if he is trying to live a righteous life, he chose that Jezebel over me!" Tears began to flow down her cheek, but it was mostly out of anger. She continued to watch DeTroyt talk with LaShae in her car. Thinking out loud again, Erica stated, "I can remember when, before *she* ever existed, DeTroyt and I would have the best of times together. Now ever since this freak accident where he decided to play God, it's been Shae this! Shae that! Ugh, just you wait 'till I see that whore again. I'm going to make her life a living hell and DeTroyt won't be anywhere around to save her. Not to mention that little brat of his… She still has no clue who her mother is, but I just might help her find that out." She smirked.

On their way home, LaShae couldn't help but feel that something wasn't quite right. Having second thoughts about him following them, she called DeTroyt's cell phone but there was no answer. Little did she know, these feelings were the beginning of total chaos.

Chapter Seventeen

MyChele

FAMILY CHAOS/REVENGE

Monday 7:45 a.m.

The day for MyChele started out normal, as she would call it. Her cell phone rang constantly and people were forever knocking on her door. *Wow! I feel important for a change.*

After what seemed like hours of conversations, MyChele was finally able to get herself together to head into the office. She grabbed a quick breakfast and cleaned the kitchen just in case if someone else dropped by unannounced, she wouldn't be embarrassed.

For a couple of weeks after Keven's death, MyChele went into a state of depression. She didn't answer her phone calls or reply to messages of any kind. She didn't want visitors and she wanted nothing to do with social media. Today, she was due back to work and she was very excited about it; she felt refreshed.

MyChele gathered her briefcase and purse to head out; however, when she opened the door, she came face to face with *him*. All she could do was gasp for air as the blows came harder and harder. MyChele grunted and fell to the floor as the last hard blow was to her head. *Thump.* Then, he was gone.

About an hour went by before anyone even realized that MyChele was not seated at her normal seat in the conference room where their daily meetings were held.

"Has anyone seen or heard from MyChele today?" asked one of her coworkers. "It's not like her to miss any days or not call if she wasn't going to be here."

Everyone shook their heads no and mumbled, "I haven't heard from her."

Jack said, "Well, you know her brother, Keven, was murdered a few days ago…"

"Ummph, you know that wasn't her *real* brother," retorted Charlotte. "She doesn't have any *real* family and from what she told me, he was more than what you would call a *brother*."

Charlotte Welch was in her mid thirties and was divorced with three children. Not only was she short in stature, but in temperament as well which made it hard for her to be in any relationship. Of course men thought that she was pretty, but not as beautiful as MyChele. Charlotte was very good at her job, but she was lazy when it came to presenting new ideas. She would come up with slogans and graphs and things of that nature, but before she would put it all together as a project, she'd pass it on to MyChele for a little "help" as she called it. She wanted to get everyone to believe that MyChele was stealing her ideas, but her plan always backfired. Little did Charlotte know, hidden cameras were installed in her office by their manager, Lindsey, so they could catch Charlotte whenever she was up to something. MyChele was sworn to secrecy about this little setup.

When she finished making her statement, everyone was staring at her in disbelief. They knew that Charlotte was extremely jealous of MyChele because of the attention that she got at work, but nonetheless, the comment was uncalled for.

Just then, there was a knock at the door and the receptionist entered the room. After hearing what she had to say, the room was silent. "The police," she continued, "stated that she was beaten pretty badly and was lying in a pool of blood, left for dead. Right now, she's in the ICU at Central."

Finally, Michael, a dear friend and coworker, asked, "Who found her if she lives by herself?"

Everyone turned to him as if to ask how he knew that bit of information.

He saw the looks he was being given and replied, "She told me this not too long ago, guys, come on." Turning back to the receptionist, he waited on an answer.

"A neighbor found her after she saw a suspicious car speed away. According to the police, MyChele's neighbor stated that she walks her dog at the same time every morning which is the same time that MyChele leaves for work. MyChele's car was still in the yard and her door was wide open, which was extremely odd for her."

"Or so the story goes…" Charlotte broke in yet again. This time, no one paid any attention to her.

Michael was the first to get up. "I'm going to see her. Would anyone like to join me?"

With that, the entire conference room, with the exception of Charlotte, got up from their comfortable chairs and headed toward the door.

Jasmyn ——————————————————————— **Monday 9:02 a.m.**

Jasmyn rose early to do her exercises. Afterward, she showered and sat on her balcony in her robe, drinking her orange juice, eating her bagel, and enjoying the fresh morning breeze.

She noticed a strange vehicle parked across the street from her home; the windows were tinted extremely dark and the driver's side window was slightly ajar. Jasmyn, already knowing what to expect, froze in her seat.

Without warning, shots rang out. Jasmyn felt the graze from the bullet as it passed her left ear and shattered the patio door that led to the kitchen. She hid behind the wall of her balcony that, thank God, was solid brick or else she would have been dead by now. Jasmyn saw drops of blood on the concrete that was apparently coming from her grazed ear. She desperately wanted to make a move for the inside but felt it better to stay put.

God, the pain!

The shots continued for what seemed like forever, but in actuality, the entire scene lasted for a full minute. Afterward, she heard screeching of tires and then… silence. The car was gone.

In the distance, she could hear sirens. Someone had obviously called and reported gunfire on her behalf. She reached for her phone that was underneath the table where she was sitting prior to the gunfire. Also underneath the table, Jasmyn noticed a brick wrapped in white paper. Careful not to touch it, she rolled it over with her phone in order to read the note.

YOU AND YOUR PRECIOUS LITTLE PEACHES BETTER BEWARE. I'M WATCHING YOU!

Several officers arrived on the scene and were questioning neighbors. Officers Simpson and Johnson made their way to Jasmyn's apartment to question her. Jasmyn was so nervous she didn't know what to do. Her heart was still racing, blood was dripping from her ear, her hair was a mess, and she was breaking out in cold sweats. She was in such shock that she didn't even realize the pain that she was in. Officer Simpson, even though he was there to do his job, saw what a mess she was in and led her to the nearest seat that he saw. Once she was seated and after introducing themselves to her, they went right into questioning. "We understand that there was a report of gunfire at this address."

Jasmyn nodded her head yes.

"Ma'am, can you state your name?"

"Sure. It's Jasmyn. J-a-s-m-y-n Gipson with a 'p'," she replied.

"What happened here this morning?" asked Officer Simpson. His partner, Officer Johnson, was jotting down information as Jasmyn spoke. In the meantime, another squad car pulled up along with the paramedics.

Jasmyn's street was pretty busy for a Monday morning. Reporters were already trying to get the scoop on the morning shooting in the villa, but thank goodness the police had already barricaded the area. Jasmyn couldn't help but think of all the attention coming her way. She didn't like it one bit, especially if it wasn't dealing with her boutique. She wanted this attack to be kept as quietly as possible, but she soon realized this was very major and everyone was watching her.

She began explaining to both officers what had happened out on the balcony. She also presented the brick with the note attached. Officer Johnson wanted her to describe the car as best as she remembered. Jasmyn described the car as a dark colored car with dark tinted windows. She explained that everything happened so fast that she really didn't focus on the type of car it was.

"Did you get a good look at the driver?" asked Officer Simpson.

Getting frustrated, Jasmyn answered, "No, I couldn't see the person's face. The window was cracked only a little. I was so stunned by what happened... it's all a blur." Jasmyn, resting her face in her hands, began to sob uncontrollably.

The second set of officers that pulled up were investigating the skid marks of the car. They also found shell casings on the ground that looked to be from a semi-automatic weapon. The officers collected what they thought to be evidence and started loading up. The paramedics checked Jasmyn's ear and treated it for minor wounds. Her arm was placed in a sling because she sprained it when she dove from the chair to the concrete balcony floor while dodging bullets.

The chief officer, Officer Dunbar, arranged for an unmarked car to patrol her house daily until this person was caught and just in case he decided to come back to finish the job.

After a while, the paramedics and police left Jasmyn in peace. She sat in the same spot on the couch where Office Simpson led her to half an hour ago. Tears began to roll down her cheeks as she thanked God again and again for sparing her life. It was then that she heard her cell phone chirping in the distance. She wanted to get up to check it, but she was frozen in that spot on the couch. Instead, Jasmyn decided to lie down where she was to try and relax. With her arm in a sling, it was a difficult task to be on her side and it took her a minute to get comfortable. "Finally," she said. Grabbing the remote from the end table, she turned on the television only to see her face plastered across the screen.

"...And yet another mid morning attack in the Marion area," stated the anchor woman. "This time, it was boutique owner Jasmyn Gipson of Gipson Jewelry and Designs that narrowly escaped with her life. Sources say an unidentified gunman opened fire on Gipson as she sat on the balcony of her apartment complex this morning. No one has come forth at this time as a witness in the shooting, but police were called to the scene after gunshots were heard. We will keep you updated on the latest news of the gunman. I'm Kasey Cherr—"
Click.

Jasmyn turned off the television. "I need a vacation," she said, rubbing her temple. She was in too much pain to move off of the couch, so she thought what better way to start relaxing even if it is on her all plush white couch in her overly white living room. Jasmyn managed to get comfortable and before long, dozed off.

Kaleb ————————————————————— **Monday 8:55 a.m.**

LaShae awoke from somewhat of a restful night. Even though the rest of her night went smoothly, she just couldn't shake that feeling that something was terribly wrong.

She showered, dressed, then cooked breakfast. She decided to get Kaleb up last since he was easier to get dressed, unlike females.

"Kaleb, honey," LaShae called out to him as she entered his bedroom. No answer. She called to him again; this time there was a movement, but not much.

"Kaleb?" LaShae pulled back the covers only to see her baby boy shaking, sweating, and foaming at the mouth.

"Oh my God! Kaleb!" She picked him up and ran toward the living room for her keys and purse. Kaleb was trembling so much that she almost dropped him.

She opened the front door and headed toward her car then she stopped dead in her tracks. "What the…?" All four tires on her car were flat. "Who would…? Jesus, I don't have time for this now!" LaShae exclaimed as she went back inside. She laid Kaleb on the couch and dialed, yet again, 911.

"911, what's your emergency," said the operator.

"My son. He's having a seizure and I… I don't know what to do. Please help me!" There was a surprising calmness to her voice.

"Okay, ma'am. Just make sure that you protect his head and do not put your fingers in his mouth. May I have your address please?"

LaShae provided her address and waited for paramedics to arrive. The dispatcher stayed on the line with her as they both waited. "Oh my goodness. This feels like deja vu."

The dispatcher talked to LaShae to keep her mind steady. She periodically asked about Kaleb's conditions in which LaShae would reply that nothing had changed.

It only took three minutes for the paramedics to get to her house. She flung open the door to let them in. "He's in the living room on the couch," she told them. LaShae thanked the dispatcher for hanging in there with her and disconnected the call.

They followed her into the living room where they immediately began to work on Kaleb. They gave him enough anticonvulsant medication to get him to the hospital. The paramedics placed Kaleb on the gurney, strapped him in, and wheeled him onto the ambulance. Because LaShe had four flat tires, she was allowed to ride in the ambulance with Kaleb.

On the way to the hospital, LaShae called Jasmyn, but there was no answer. Even though she was angry with her, this was her grandchild and she at least needed to know what was going on with him. "Oh, Mama," she heard herself say, right above a whisper.

She tried her again, but Jasmyn's phone rang five times before her voicemail picked up. "Mama, where the hell are you?" she questioned under her breath in frustration before being prompted to leave a message. They arrived at the hospital a little after she had left the message for her mother.

Running beside Kaleb as they rushed him down the hall, she couldn't help but think what she would do if she were to lose him too. She had already buried his father last week, and she couldn't stand the thought of having to possibly bury Kaleb too. *No, not my baby!*

They rushed through the doors and down the hall to an empty room where the doctors were waiting to work on Kaleb. They motioned for LaShae to stay out. From the hallway she watched as they put a tube here, and stuck a needle there, and hooked up wires all over him. "Oh, Kaleb. I am so sorry," she said right above a whisper. All she could do was stand in the doorway and watch them work on her son.

LaShae, never hearing footsteps coming up behind her, jumped when she felt an arm slide around her shoulder. When she looked up, she breathed a sigh of relief. "DeTroyt, what are you doing here?" she asked, shocked to see him. The expression must have shown on her face because his smile quickly vanished.

He stepped back a little before responding. "Well, I was on my way over to your house when I saw the ambulance leaving so I followed it. I hope you don't mind."

LaShae quickly gave him a questionable look. "Why were you coming by? Is something wrong?'

DeTroyt decided not to reveal the real reason he was coming over to her house was because, just minutes before, he saw on the news that Jasmyn had been shot at while sitting on her balcony. This was not the time. "Never mind that. What happened to Kaleb? Is he going to be alright?"

LaShae's eyes were looking past DeTroyt toward the doctor; she was weak in the knees. DeTroyt noticed her gaze and turned in the direction of the doctor. She couldn't see in, but she could imagine what was going on behind these curtains. As the door was closing, she heard one of the doctors say, "Time of death…."

"NO!" LaShae screamed, rushing past the doctor and through the door that he'd just come out of, startling the remaining staff inside. "NO! My baby! Kaleb!" She snatched the cover off of him, trying to make him talk to her. She wanted to see his eyes. She felt DeTroyt by her side as always and as always, he was praying. LaShae didn't feel like praying. She didn't want to talk to God. He took her son away from her! And for what reason? Kaleb had never done anything. "He's just a baby, God! He's just a baby… my baby!" she wailed.

Chapter Eighteen

Kaleb

THE MIRACLE

The doctors left the room so that they could be alone to talk to Kaleb for the last time.

"I'll see you in the hallway, Ms. Wilson… whenever you are ready," Dr. Jackson said before leaving the room.

"I'll never be ready. I'm not leaving his side," she told Dr. Jackson matter-of-factly.

DeTroyt assured him that they would indeed speak with him but to give them a few minutes. Dr. Jackson agreed and continued through the door.

Kaleb's little body was still warm, not yet cold as she would think a corpse would be. *A corpse,* she thought. "This is my baby. The precious little boy that I was so excited to be carrying. The overwhelming joy that I felt when I looked at him for the first time. My baby, listening to his first works, and answering his first question." Her voice trailed off and all DeTroyt could hear was the sound of sobbing. DeTroyt rushed to her side but never stopped praying.

The tears never stopped coming as she reflected on the last five years of his life.

She could hear DeTroyt still praying but she couldn't quite make out what he was saying, but whatever it was, she didn't want to interrupt.

DeTroyt was a great friend, and she was really glad that they bumped into each other. She had to laugh because it was more like crashing into each other, but nevertheless, he was a great guy. Erica just didn't know what she had and to think how jealous she was of LaShae. Ha! Erica was a stone-cold knockout who just wasn't aware of her worth.

LaShae felt a slight tickle in the palm of her hand, or at least she thought she did. She opened the hand that held Kaleb's and stared at it as though she was hypnotized. Nothing happened. She wanted to say something to DeTroyt about it, but at the same time, she didn't want to disturb his prayer for what seemed to be an illusion. LaShae glanced quickly out of the corner of her eye just to see if DeTroyt had gotten a glimpse at what had just happened. His back was to her and he was praying to the walls.

She quickly turned back to Kaleb. "Come on, baby, tickle my palm again. Please Kaleb, don't let Mommy think she's crazy," she whispered.

She waited. Nothing.

She whispered again, this time in desperation. "Kaleb, baby, I know that I just felt you tickle my palm. I'm not crazy. Come on, sweetie."

Again, she waited. Nothing.

She was so focused on Kaleb that she didn't even notice that DeTroyt had stopped praying and was standing next to her. He placed a hand on her shoulder as if to say everything will be okay.

"LaShae, wh—"

"DeTroyt, did you see that?" LaShae asked in disbelief.

"Yeah, I did," he said even more in disbelief than she was.

Kaleb's arm moved. Was it just his final reflexes that they always said a dead person has?

"DeTroyt! He moved! I'm not crazy, am I?" LaShae asked out of desperation.

Without answering her, DeTroyt made his way to the other side of Kaleb's bed to get a better look. "Lord, God," he started in an amazingly low soft tone. "I know that you work miracles, but this, Lord, is beyond anything that I have ever seen."

Kaleb began gasping for air and then a soft moan came out which sounded more like a whine. DeTroyt, staring down at Kaleb, saw the fluttering of his eyelids, and so did LaShae. Kaleb's eyes opened, focusing on DeTroyt, yet he looked confused. Then he turned his gaze to LaShae.

"Mommy," he managed in a very raspy voice. His throat was extremely dry from the tube.

LaShae was speechless, amazed, and confused all at the same time. Tears began to flow and she did not know whether to hold him or stare at him. She chose the latter.

DeTroyt ran out of the room to get Dr. Jackson who, when he entered the room, was more amazed than anyone. All of the previous doctors and nurses that left Kaleb dead were all astounded. Dr. Jackson began examining Kaleb over and over again only to find that Kaleb was as healthy as he could be. Despite the astonished look on everyone's faces, Dr. Jackson announced that all was well with Kaleb, but they were going to place him in a room for overnight observation.

"I don't understand, Dr.," LaShae said, pulling him aside. "He was dead, not breathing. What is this? What happened to him?"

Dr. Jackson had no answer at the moment, but he promised to research and let her know.

After getting Kaleb settled into a room, LaShae called her mother again to see where she was. In all that was going on, DeTroyt forgot to tell his real reason for coming over in the first place. He decided this would be a great time to do so.

"Shae, I need to tell you something."

LaShae gave a look of terror, but she braced herself as he continued. "The reason that I was coming over to your house this morning was to tell you that your mom was involved in a shooting incident."

"What?" she exclaimed.

"She's okay though. The gunman purposely shot at her as she sat on her balcony. We still do not know who did it, but she was pretty shaken up. Per the news report, she is fine, but was definitely the gunman's target. I've tried to call her, but she is not answering her phone. I came over to your place to see if she was with you, but after seeing your car on flat and the ambulance leaving your house, I could only expect the worst."

"Oh my goodness!" was all that LaShae could say. Grabbing her cell phone, she attempts to call Jasmyn again.

Jasmyn answered on the first ring. "Hello?"

"Mama! Thank God! Are you alright? DeTroyt told me what happened. He said that it was all over the news." LaShae felt her blood pumping and had to catch herself. She fell quiet long enough for Jasmyn to answer her questions, then she filled her mom in on what happened with Kaleb.

"I am at the hospital, but I am downstairs. I will explain everything to you when I get up there in a few minutes. What room is he in?"

"Okay, Mama, we are in room 312," LaShae said before hanging up.

DeTroyt told LaShae that he would stay with her until Jasmyn got into the room. They decided to walk down the hall to meet Jasmyn at the elevators while Kaleb slept.

Heading toward the elevators to meet Jasmyn, LaShae saw a patient lying in bed that caught her eye. "Mychele?" LaShae was about to enter the room when an officer, who appeared out of nowhere, blocked her entrance.

"May I help you with something, ma'am?" he asked in a low husky voice. His attitude showed no sign of kindness.

Startled at the officer's reaction, LaShae jumped back into DeTroyt. "Well, yes… yes, you can. That's my best friend there. Would you mind telling me what happened to her and why you're guarding her door?" She took a few steps back, waiting for him to respond.

"You're her best friend, huh? So do you have a name, *best friend?*" he asked more in a sarcastic tone than a friendly one.

LaShae gave him her name with an attitude. "Yes, I am her best friend. Do you mind telling me what happened to her or should I go and ask her myself?"

"Hold on now, young lady. You need to answer a few questions for me before I tell you anything about this patient."

DeTroyt saw the officer reaching for his handcuffs. "Now wait a minute," DeTroyt interjected. "She just wants to know what happened to her. We are here with LaShae's five year old son down the hall and just happened to pass this room as she was walking me out. She's not trying to start any trouble. She's just a concerned friend is all."

"Who are you?" the officer asked DeTroyt.

"My name is DeTroyt Maning, and I am also a friend of MyChele."

The officer wouldn't budge from the door nor would he allow them to ask anymore questions. He motioned for them to go on. Disappointed, they did. LaShae tried to argue her point, however, DeTroyt pushed her down the hall toward the elevators.

When they arrived at the elevators, Jasmyn was coming off. LaShae ran over to her mother and gave her a big hug. "Mama, I am so glad that you are okay."

Jasmyn hugged her back. "I'm fine, honey. How is Kaleb?" She turned to DeTroyt and gave him a hug as well. Jasmyn thanked him for staying with LaShae until she got there. LaShae told Jasmyn what room Kaleb was in and that she would be in there in a moment. With that, Jasmyn headed toward Kalebs room.

Turning back to DeTroyt, LaShae thanked him for being with her and assured him that she would be okay. He gently kissed her on the cheek and stepped into the elevator. She watched as the doors closed and slowly began walking back toward Kaleb's room. She placed her hand on the side of her face where DeTroyt kissed her and the biggest smile spread across her face. His lips were so soft and gentle, like a baby's kiss.

Without warning, the officer who was guarding MyChele's door before, handcuffed LaShae and began reading her rights to her. *This surely got her attention.*

"What are you doing?" she protested. "Let me go!"

The unnamed officer was getting a little rough with her. "Miss Wilson, you are under arrest for the murder of Keven Mitchell and the assault against Miss MyChele Tanner," he said with certainty.

"Wait, what? You can't arrest me because I didn't do anything! Now let me go!" she yelled between struggles.

Visitors began to peek out of their rooms and the doctors and nurses began to stare as well. She regretted that DeTroyt left since he had to get Vicki from school. Jasmyn came out of Kaleb's room just as the officer finished reading LaShae her rights.

"My partner is on his way up," he stated. "So you just need to remain calm, Miss Wilson." The officer was still handling LaShae a bit rough, at least that was how it seemed to Jasmyn who had just stepped out of Kaleb's room to see what all the commotion was about.

"Officer! What on earth is going on here? Why do you have my daughter in handcuffs?" Jasmyn was by no means in the mood to be nice to anyone especially after what happened to her that morning. The officer looked at Jasmyn with cold stone eyes.

"I asked what's going on here!?" she asked, this time grabbing the officer by the arm.

"Mama, please calm down," LaShae requested. She tried to assure Jasmyn that she was okay and they would get to the bottom of this soon. "Excuse me, officer," LaShae said. "My son is in the room down the hall recovering from epilepsy. I have no idea what you're talking about. I've been with him all day long. I do not know about an assault against Mychele which is why I was asking you earlier what happened to her. Why would I attack my best friend? If anything, you need to be trying to find out who attacked her because it wasn't me! I don't mind going 'downtown,' as you call it, and I don't mind answering whatever questions that you may have, but what I do mind is being falsely accused of a crime that I didn't commit. Especially murder!"

"Murder!" exclaimed Jasmyn.

"Yes, Mama. Not only is he accusing me of assaulting MyChele, but I'm also being accused of murdering Keven! All I want to know is why?" LaShae was beyond angry, but she tried to stay as calm as possible.

"Why don't you tell me why, Miss Wilson?" said the police officer. "I would really like to know."

"Yes, *we* would really like to know," came another voice. LaShae turned around to see a second cop standing there with his head down scribbling something on his notepad. She almost fainted when she saw his face. *Stephon Knight! What on earth was he doing dressed like a policeman?*

"Mama, can you please go back to the room with Kaleb?" she asked Jasmyn. Jasmyn wanted to protest, but LaShae insisted that she would be fine. After she heard the door to Kaleb's room close, she turned back to Stephon.

"What the hell are you doing here?" she asked him furiously.

With a smirk, he announced, "Well, I'm here to take you in, Miss Wilson." He walked over to her and stood looking down at her. "Yes, Miss Wilson, I am here to take you," he said pointing with his index finger, "for a ride." Stephon stood a few inches over LaShae.

"I will never go anywhere with you, Stephon," Shae said firmly. Had he been a little closer, she would have sealed her comment with a nice spitball.

"Stephon? My name is Officer Johnson. You have me mixed up with someone else, my dear," he stated nonchalantly.

"You can pretend to be who you want to be, but I'm not stupid and I'm not riding anywhere with you," she stated matter-of-factly. She tried to walk away, but she forgot that she was handcuffed.

"Oh no, you don't!" he said, grabbing her forearm. "I do believe the elevators are this way, ma'am."

LaShae tried to pull away.

"Do I need to book you for resisting arrest as well?"

"Okay, alright," she said reluctantly. "But, Kaleb, my son, is in the room down the hall recovering from a seizure. I would like to go and say goodbye to him please." She wiggled her hands. "Can these handcuffs be removed? At least until we leave for the station? I don't want my son to see me in these things. I promise, I won't run."

After letting out a sigh, Officer Johnson motioned for his partner to unlock the handcuffs but he kept a grip on LaShae.

They walked down the hall to Kaleb's room with Officer Johnson close behind her. He waited outside the door for LaShae. She explained to Jasmyn what was going on.

Walking over to Kaleb's bed and taking his hand, LaShae said, "The officer that came up when you were in the hallway, his eyes… they look so familiar to me."

"Really." Jasmyn stated.

"Yes, really. I mean the more I look at him, the more it seems as though I know him, not in a hateful way though." She shook the thought off and started focusing on Kaleb. She rubbed his hand and forehead. He was sleeping peacefully. She then turned her attention to her mother.

"Mama, what happened to you this morning?" LaShae came and sat down next to Jamyn.

"I got your message, but at the same time, I was still shaky about what happened and just couldn't muster up the strength to call you."

LaShae could see a difference in her mother's demeanor just from speaking about it.

"Mama, you don't have to…"

"I don't even think *I* am clear on what happened," Jasmyn continued. "All I remember is coming out onto the balcony after my shower and seeing a strange car parked across the street. I never looked away, so I saw him when he rolled the window down and pointed a gun in my direction. He commenced shooting. Thank God I was only grazed by one of the bullets on my ear. I dodged every way I could. When I dived onto the balcony floor, I landed on my arm, hence the sling." Jasmyn paused for a moment and rubbed her arm. "The neighbors, I'm assuming, called the police. When they got there, they asked me if I saw the guy's face, but all I remember seeing was the barrel of a gun."

"Oh my goodness, Mama!" she said, grabbing her mother tightly. "I could've lost you *and* Kaleb today."

"I know, baby, but you didn't," Jasmyn assured. "We are still here, together."

Just then, the door opened and Officer Johnson came in. "I hate to interrupt you ladies, but I really need Miss Wilson to come with me now. We have a few questions to ask her." He smirked as he held the door open for LaShae to come through.

"Mama," LaShae whispered. "If I'm not back in an hour, call the police." She gave Jasmyn another hug and Kaleb a quick kiss on his forehead.

Jasmyn looked confused, but agreed. LaShae turned and gave the same smirky smile back to him and proceeded through the door and down the hall toward the elevators.

Before Officer Johnson closed the door, Jasmyn noticed how he was looking at Kaleb. There was a bit of hurt in his eyes, as if he wanted to say something, but couldn't. He noticed Jasmyn's confused expression and quickly, but quietly, closed the door. He caught up with LaShae who was already waiting at the elevator.

"See?" she taunted. "If I was trying to run away, I would have taken the stairs." However, she knew if she tried to get away, the big bad officer would have tackled her before she got off the first flight of stairs.

Moments later, LaShae was in the backseat of a squad car. She was being taken downtown for questioning in the murder/assault case of her fiancè and best friend. After fifteen minutes of riding, LaShae realized that they hadn't made it to the station yet even though it was only five minutes away from the hospital. It would have been ten with heavy traffic but traffic was very light. Instead, Officer Johnson took a turn down an alley where he brought the car to an abrupt stop. Now she was nervous.

"Why are we stopping? This isn't the police station!" LaShae, even though she knew it was useless, tried to wiggle her way out of the handcuffs.

Officer Johnson slowly turned around and stared at her through the gated window. "LaShae," he started just above a whisper. "It's me, Keven."

LaShae stopped wiggling long enough to take a closer look. That was what was so familiar about his eyes. It couldn't be. *Keven's dead.* "You're lying!" she screamed. "My Keven is dead, and you killed him!"

Keven got out of the car and came around to her side. He opened the door and squatted down next to her so that she could get a closer look. "LaShae, I am Keven, your fiancè and Kaleb's father."

"I don't believe you!" she yelled trying to kick him at the same time.

"Shae, please stop!" he demanded. He grabbed her legs and demanded that she slide over so that he could get in the car. "Listen, I know that is hard for you to swallow, but it's the truth. I am Keven, and I am alive."

"If you are alive, who did I bury? Huh? Who was that?" she screamed through her tears.

Keven wanted to comfort her, but because he only had a few moments to let her know what was going on, he had to move quickly. He knew that if he were to give into his emotions right now, everything he had worked to uncover up until this point would be null and void. "Baby, listen. Nobody knows what I am telling you or even knows that I am alive except the precinct. It has to stay that way. My cover cannot be blown or this would blow up in my face. So once I tell you the truth, I don't want to hear it again. Understood?" he asked, cradling her face in the palm of his hand.

"Yes," she managed to get out between sniffs. Keven wiped her tears away as he had done the night that he had proposed to her.

She sat quietly and waited.

"I was placed on a very important, but extremely dangerous assignment. The assignment? You and Stephon."

"You know a-about Stephon?" she asked in disbelief.

"Sweetheart, I know everything," he stated. "It's my job to know everything." He paused for a moment before continuing. "Shae, I have been following you and Stephon ever since I found out that he was looking for you. I know the past that you have together, but that's not what concerns me. What concerns me is the involvement of our friend, MyChele."

"MyChele?" she asked in shock. "What does she have to do with any of this?"

Keven sighed before answering. "We have been following MyChele for a very long time too. She is involved in an extremely dangerous, yet very important case which leads back to you and Stephon when you were fifteen years old. It seems she is the reason that Stephon 'found' you. She knew that you had planned to run away from home; she just needed to be sure of the day and time. With that information, she was able to send Stephon out to find you and he did. Now, his operation had already caused another young lady her life, but no one knew that she was dead. Well, you fit her profile perfectly which was why you were chosen. MyChele knew what happened to the young lady, but she refused to go to the police in order to protect her cousin, Stephon. Instead, she helped him cover it up.

When your mother started searching for you through the news media and pictures, Stephon and MyChele got a little worried. Even though they were young, they were smart in handling the situation. The heat began to rise when the parents of the deceased young lady began searching for their daughter as well. The truth finally came out when Stephon's workers really paid attention to who you were and realized that you were not that deceased young lady. Some of them wanted to come forward, but they were too afraid that they would end up like Shontae. When the detective found you and brought you home, Mychele decided that it was time to move back home to her parents'. This is why she is here now and has been here since then."

Keven paused to allow LaShae to take in all of this information. Her face gave a look of uncertainty, but her eyes were full of pain. He felt bad. Not only did he have to fake his death to solve this case (since he had gotten too close to the subject), but he had to tell her that the girl that she had been calling her best friend for over fifteen years had actually used her to benefit the likes of others.

"Keven," LaShae finally said. "Is that it?"

Shifting uneasily in the seat, he replied, "No, there's more."

"Then please continue." There was an awkward calmness in her voice. It was as though she was numb and it was coming through loud and clear.

Keven cleared his throat. "At the time of the investigation, MyChele has already committed perjury, by attempted murder on a little old lady and assault with a deadly weapon."

"What? You must have the wrong woman cause my friend, *our* friend, has done none of that," LaShae stated matter of factly. "I mean it's bad enough that you are accusing her of being involved in a murder, but for those things too?"

He could tell that this was beginning to be too much for her, but he was in too deep to stop. "No, we have the right one alright. MyChele is also into drugs an—"

"Drugs!" she interrupted. "Now I know you're crazy!"

"Yes, drugs, and we were afraid that you would fall into one of her traps again unbeknownst."

"I'm not believing any of this bull. MyChele is not involved in drugs nor did she do that other stuff you said that she did." LaShae was angrier now than she was when she first saw him.

"Shae, wait…" Keven started.

"Look, just take me back to the hospital or to the police station. You have ten minutes left before my mother calls the police." With that, she turned her back to him and faced outside. Keven didn't have a choice but to get out of the backseat and back into the driver seat. He knew that she was going to have a hard time receiving what he had to say, but this was more than expected.

How was he going to convince her that he was telling the truth? There had to be a way…

Chapter Nineteen

La Shae

TRUTH OR LIE

Keven and LaShae arrive back at the hospital just as Jasmyn was walking up the hall, cell phone in hand. "I was just about to call them, Shae. Are you alright?"

LaShae looked over at Keven, who slightly shook his head "no", before responding to her mother. "Yes, Mama, I'm fine. He took me for questioning just like he said he would. It just took longer than I expected, but everything is fine and I am free to go. Isn't that right, Officer Johnson?" LaShae turned back to him with a smirk on her face.

Keven stared at her in disbelief. He couldn't believe that she was taking everything that he told her for a joke. He decided to go along with her charade, at least while in front of Jasmyn. He smiled and replied, "That is right, Miss Wilson. You are *indeed* a free woman. Thank you for your time and cooperation." He tilted his hat toward the both of them. "Evening, ladies," he said before departing towards the elevators. He stopped and said something to the other guard at MyChele's door then continued walking toward the elevators.

He was being sarcastic and LaShae knew it, yet she let him walk out of her life again, without further explanation as to why he did what he did.

"Come on, Mama, let's go back to the room," she said, leading Jasmyn back to Kaleb's room. "How is Kaleb doing?" she asked, trying to shift the awkwardness.

Jasmyn, still a little puzzled as to what just transpired, answered, "Kaleb is doing fine. DeTroyt came back and is with him now. He brought Vicki back with him. I hope that was okay."

"Um, sure. Yes, that was fine." It was not that she didn't want DeTroyt or Vicki there at the hospital, it was the mere fact that she was just told that her fiancè was alive and that she had seen him in the flesh as an undercover... cop? She loved Keven and she knew that she always will. Ever since his death, LaShae has been trying her best to move forward, but it's been hard, extremely hard. And now this? Granted, it had only been a few days since she buried him. *What am I supposed to do with this? she wondered.*

She was so confused. She realized that she met DeTroyt months ago at a very vulnerable time in her life. She was hurt, confused, and hated her baby's father. And once again, he left her and a few days later decided that he wanted back in? This time, he even went as far as to fake his death and disguised himself as her enemy, Stephon. He also falsely accused her best friend of fifteen years of the unimaginable. It was almost a shame to ask what he will think of next.

Arriving at Kaleb's room, LaShae put all of this new found drama behind her as she entered.

"Hey, Ms. Shae," Vicki said as she ran to hug her.

"Well, hello, Vicki. It's good to see you," she replied, hugging her back.

"You too," she said. Her smile vanished when she looked back at Kaleb who was sleeping peacefully.

"Kaleb's going to be okay, right, Ms. Shae? Daddy and I have been praying for him."

"Then I am more than certain that Kaleb will be just fine," LaShae assured her, giving her a tight squeeze.

LaShae spoke to DeTroyt and went over to sit beside Kaleb's bedside. They laughed and talked. Kaleb, who seemed to be doing a lot better than before, woke up occasionally to talk, but the incidents of the day never came up. No Keven, no MyChele, no arrests.

The time came for visiting hours to be over and DeTroyt and Vicki decided to call it a night. Jasmyn had left about an hour earlier to get some rest. "Thank you for everything, DeTroyt. You've been such a great help to me, to us," she added, pointing to Kaleb. "With the loss of his dad, it's really been rough for the both of us. Thank you too, Vicki, for being such a great friend to Kaleb." They said their goodbyes and left the room.

Once alone, she had to wonder if she was dreaming earlier about Keven and if the things he had said about MyChele were actually true. There was no way that LaShae could get into MyChele's room to talk with her because she was being closely guarded.

"Dammit, Keven!" LaShae exclaimed under her breath. "How did I let you do this to me again?" LaShae stared out the window in Kaleb's room, looking out across the city and pondering that thought. A commotion in the parking lot caught her attention. She squinted to make out who it was and from what she could see, it looked like Keven in his Officer Johnson disguise and…

"Oh, no! DeTroyt!" she exclaimed, running out of the room. When LaShae made it to the parking lot, Keven was walking back toward the ER doors. He stopped in front of her and said, "You better watch your boy! He ain't all he claims to be."

"What is that supposed to mean?" she asked, definitely confused now. If she couldn't trust DeTroyt, then who else was she supposed to turn to?

Instead of explaining what he meant, he gestured for her to come back inside the hospital. She followed his lead.

"Hey!" she yelled. "What was that all about?" she demanded, trying to keep up to his pace and now causing a scene.

"I don't want to talk about it right now!" he replied sternly.

LaShae stopped in her tracks. "You listen to me," she said, grabbing Officer Johnson by the arm. He couldn't help but stop. "DeTroyt has been nothing but good to me, and I have every right to know what's going on here. He is my friend, and if he is in some sort of trouble, I need to know!"

Keven calmly walked closer to her and as quietly as he could without making a scene, he replied, "LaShae, this is official police business. You don't need to know anything. I choose to tell you things and all I am telling you right now is to watch your boy. He is not all that he claims to be." With that, Keven walked away. LaShae, still upset and confused, followed close behind, not saying anything.

They made it back to the room just as Kaleb was waking up. LaShae stopped Keven at the door. "Listen, Officer Johnson, uh Keven, or whatever your name is…" She was still not convinced that he was who he had claimed to be earlier that day to her. "I would rather you not come into this room ever. I do not want my son to go through anything that will cause him to be stressed out. He has suffered enough."

"LaShae, how could you still not believe me? I've told you why I did what I did and I've apologized for it. What more do you want?" he asked.

"I want you to leave us alone," she stated as she entered the room and shut the door behind her.

Keven stood there for a moment before leaving to head to his post. It was his turn to guard MyChele's door; however, he longed to see his son. Though he was right down the hall from him, he seemed so far away.

Chapter Twenty

La Shae

SIX MONTHS LATER

"It's been six months, DeTroyt. Six months! There has been no justice for what was done to Keven, my mom, my son, nor MyChele, let alone who flattened my tires! What's wrong with these people? Can't they see what's going on here?" she yelled.

DeTroyt got up from the kitchen bar and made his way to her. He placed his arms ever so gently around her and embarrassed her like a man who was truly in love. Softly, he began to speak. "Baby, look. Please don't do this to yourself. I'm sure that they are doing all that they can to get to the bottom of these attacks. Yes, Keven and MyChele's killer is still out there, but we have to believe that the person will get caught or turn themselves in. It is out of our hands."

He pulled back from the embrace and lifted her face toward his. "LaShae Wilson, I love you and I refuse to let anything happen to you. We are going to put this thing before God and leave it at the altar."

LaShae looked at DeTroyt as though those three words were foreign to her. *He said that he loves me. Oh my goodness, that feels so good within my spirit and my soul. He actually loves me.*

"I thank God for you," she finally said. She pulled him closer and held him tightly. "I truly thank God for you."

She didn't want this moment to end. Just to be in his arms, she felt safe, loved, secured, and that was wonderful. "Never let me go."

DeTroyt pulled her from his embrace to look at her. He stared at her with passion in his eyes and she knew that she had that same look of desire.

"You don't ever have to worry about me letting you go anywhere. You and I were meant to happen," he stated softly.

All LaShae could do was smile.

"From day one, when I saw you in that hospital bed, even when you were stressing me out, I fell in love with your inner being. You were and still are beautiful on the inside and definitely on the outside."

Her smile grew bigger, as he continued.

"Even though our beginning was a little rocky, I thank God that I met you. I love you very much."

"I love you too," she proclaimed, pulling away. "That is why you have to go now." LaShae led him toward the door.

"Time to go?" DeTroyt asked reluctantly. "But we weren't doing anything…"

"Yes, and I would like to keep it that way." LaShae grinned sheepishly and pushed him through the front door. After kissing him on the check, she told him good night and closed the door before she changed her mind. Never had she felt so loved before, not even with Keven. She felt respected and cherished for the first time in her life. To God be all the glory.

She began to reflect on all of the bad relationships she had been in and thanked God. She thanked him for her maturity and life lessons. Had it not been for those bad relationships, she never would have learned how to appreciate the blessings that a good relationship had to offer. *What a blessing he is.*

She looked at the time and it was 9 o'clock. Kaleb was with Jasmyn so she had the entire house to herself. She wondered if she should have kicked DeTroyt out so soon. She thought about calling him back, but she was pretty sure that would lead to a lot of trouble… trouble that neither of them needed. She decided to take a long hot soak in the tub before turning in for the night.

As she walked into her bathroom, she noticed that the window was slightly ajar. She stood there and stared for a moment, backtracking what she did today. Leaving the bathroom window ajar was not one of them. LaShae looked around for any signs of disturbance in the bathroom, but she couldn't find any. Then a hard, loud knock on the front door made her jump. She was hesitant at first, but the knock came again.

LaShae started making her way toward the door when a figure met her in the hallway holding a metal object. One hit was all it would take and LaShae knew that. She was trapped, not able to get to the front door nor back into the bathroom. Her best bet? Scream! Maybe the person knocking on the other side of the door will hear the screaming and bust through the door to save her.

"Help!" she cried out. "Somebody help me, please!"

"LaShae?" came the voice on the other side of the door. It was DeTroyt. "LaShae!" He heard a thump and then silence. He kicked in the door only to be met with the same figure holding the same metal object.

To be continued......

About the author:

Lisa~Lije' Johnson, a singer/songwriter and author, is a proud native of Columbia, MS who enjoys writing and being very creative in her God-given crafts.

She first discovered her talents for both singing and -writing at a very young age and has continued to develop them over the years.

Lisa is the author of her self published book of poetry entitled "Diary of Expressions" and was one of many contributing co-authors of "Raising a Proverb 31 Woman: Self-Esteem, Self-Worth, and Self-Discovery of a Young Woman" with LaTracey Copeland Hughes.

Lisa currently resides on the Mississippi Gulf Coast and in her leisure time, she enjoys traveling and spending time with family and friends.

Be on the lookout for more publications from Lisa~Lije'. Lisa's music can be found at **www.reverbnation.com/lisaajohnson**